Faith / Leni

FAITH / LENI

Her Sweet Revenge Series - Book - #5 & #6

Mimi Barbour

Sarna Publishing

Contents

Dedication

I'm dedicating this series to my father, who we lovingly refer to as Papa John. This man has been a huge influence throughout my life. He's a smart, energetic, affectionate and very wise ninety-two-year-old man who is still going strong – likes to brag that he's only taking one pill a day. He's legally blind, but no one can tell from the way he gets around. Whenever he appears in the dining room at his lodge, people light up, and the jokes start flying.

This man brightens the day for everyone around him, and it thrills me to be his very fortunate daughter. To dedicate this new series to him is my way of telling the world that without his calm guidance and constant example, I'd never be the writer, the wife, the mother or the successful, happy woman I am today.

I love you, Papa John!

*Sadly, I lost my wonderful Papa John in 2018, and in his memory I wrote a book using him as one of the characters. It's called Special Agent Charli. So far, he seems to be reaping the best comments in the book's many reviews. Amazon Universal link: http://mybook.to/SpecialAgentCharli

Praise for Faith and Leni

"Was so glad to have Faith's story. Read first 4 books in the series (all of which I would give a 5-star rating) and having Faith with her own happy ending, after all she had been through, was icing on the cake. Looking forward to Leni's story! Have you considered giving Sam his own story?" ~ *Reviewed by Fran Kershner*

"What a gorgeous book! I'm really enamored of this series and I'm so glad the author decided to tell Faith's story (and that Leni's is next). This story continues events in the previous book, with the characteristic great writing and action-packed plot I've come to expect from Mimi Barbour. I really appreciate how strong the female characters are, whether physically or mentally or emotionally, and Faith is no different. A really lovely story that I read in one sitting (cause I just had to know how it would end!)" ~ *Reviewed by Bella*

"What a great read! Mimi Barbour has outdone herself with this sweet novella. Although a part of the Her Sweet Revenge series, this book can be read as a stand-alone, also. A very powerful story about a prostitute turned nanny and the single father that hired her to care for his newborn baby." ~ *Reviewed by Laura*

Leni – Praise:

"I definitely recommend to get this book this the 6th book in Mob Tracker Series which is certainly a terrific series with great strong, captivating characters that pull you right onto the story it's a must have book you don't want to miss I opened and couldn't put it down until finished reading." ~ *Reviewed by Diane*

"What a great end to Cassi's story! I could not put this book down until I found out how her story ended and if she finally got the truth she searched so hard for about her brother's killer. Needless to say, Mimi did not disappoint! If you haven't read any of the books in this series, you must start with book 1 and read them in order. You will not be disappointed." ~ *Reviewed by Laura*

"I have read every book Mimi has written. This is her best series. Cass has become a strong women, because of bad things in her life. She has lost too many people she loves. On a high note of defeating a crazy fighter she gets the news, the love of her life is kidnapped. I am pretty sure I got the clue where he is. Now when is the next book ready? I highly recommend Mimi's books. All are good." ~ *Reviewed by Shirleen*

"What an absolutely brilliant ending to Cassi's story. In typical fashion with this series, could not put this book down. There were so many twists and turns and unexpected events that I was holding my breath in some spots, the anticipation of what was to come was so intense! So pleased we will also get to read Faith's story! I can't get enough of these characters." ~ *Reviewed by Bella*

Also author of...

— Make an Elvis Song a Book! —
She's Not You (Book 1)
Love Me Tender (Book 2)
***

Vegas Series
— Action–Packed Thrillers! —
Vegas Series – Complete Boxed Set
Partners (Book 1)
Roll the Dice (Book 2)
Vegas Shuffle (Book 3)
High Stakes Gamble (Book 4)
Spin the Wheel (Book 5)
Let it Ride (Book 6)
***

Undercover FBI Series
— Popular & Compelling! —
Special Agent Francesca (Book 1)
Special Agent Finnegan (Book 2)
Special Agent Maximilian (Book 3)
Special Agent Kandice (Book 4)
Special Agent Booker (Book 5)
Special Agent Charli (Book 6)
Special Agent Rylee (Book 7)
Special Agent Murphy (Book 8)
Special Agent Sophia (Book #9 – to be released
in May 2020)
***

Holiday Heartwarmers Series
— Truly a Christmas favorite! —
Holiday Heartwarmers Trilogy

Please Keep Me (Book 1)
Snow Pup (Book 2)
Find Me a Home (Book 3)
Frosty the Snowman (Book 4)
Love of my Life (Book 5)
A Perfect Storm (Book 6)
***

Her Sweet Revenge Series
— She's unstoppable! —
Retaliation (Book #1)
Justice (Book #2)
Resolution (Book #3
Endings – (Book #4)
Faith (Book #5)
Leni (Book #6)
***

Single Title Series
He's My Baby (Book #1)
Christmas Runaway (Book #2)
Because You cared (Book #3)
Daddy's Mine (Book #4 – to be released in
March 2020)
***

The Best in Romance Series
Red Hot Divas (Book #1 Box Set)
Hot and Handsome (Book #2 Box Set
***

Other Titles
I'm No Angel
Hotshot Cowboy

Big Girls Don't Cry
The Surrogate's Secret
Mimi's Mix (Box Set)
'Tis the Season (Box Set)
Hearts, Flowers & Romance (Box Set)
Love, Christmas (Multi-author Box Set)
Unforgettable Romances (Multi-author Box Set)
Sweet and Sassy (Multi-author Box Set)
Unforgettable Heroes (Multi-author Box Set)
Unforgettable Christmas (Multi-author Box Set)
A Christmas She'll Remember (Multi-author Box Set)
Snowflakes and Christmas Kisses (Multi-author Box Set)
Unforgettable Valentine (Multi-author Box Set)
A Valentine She'll Remember (Multi-author Box Set)
Unforgettable Suspense (Multi-author Box Set)
Unforgettable Danger (Multi-author Box Set)
Unforgettable Trouble (Multi-author Box Set)
Unforgettable Weddings (Multi-author Box Set)
A Wedding She'll Remember (Multi-author Box Set)
Sweet and Sassy Brides (Multi-author Box Set)
Love, Christmas 2 (Multi-author Box Set)
Sweet and Sassy Suspense (Multi-author Box Set)

Unforgettable Thrills (Multi-author Box Set)
Unforgettable Passion (Multi-author Box Set)
A Romance She'll Remember (Multi-author
Box Set)
Sweet and Sassy Cinderella (Multi-author Box
Set)
Unforgettable Power (Multi-author Box Set)
Daring Protectors (Multi-author Box Set)
Unforgettable Charmers (Multi-author Box Set)
Sweet and Sassy Baby Love (Multi-author Box
Set)
Sweet and Sassy Heroes (Multi-author Box Set)
Unforgettable Intrigue (Multi-author Box Set)
Unforgettable Christmas Dreams (Multi-author
Box Set)
Sweet and Sassy Holiday (Multi-author Box
Set)
Christmas Shorts (Multi-author Box Set)
Unforgettable Temptations (Multi-author Box
Set)
Doctors in Love #2 (Multi-author Box Set)
Cute but Crazy (Multi-author Box Set)
Unforgettable Joy (Multi-author Box Set)
Sweet and Sassy Daddies (Multi-author Box
Set)
Unforgettable Joy (Multi-author Box Set)
Cute But Crazy (Multi-author Box Set)

***

Website: http://mimibarbour.com

Faith

Her Sweet Revenge Series – Book #5
by
Mimi Barbour

NYT & USA Today Best-selling author
~*~*~

Hooker turned nanny, Faith Whitely, known to her johns as Sunshine, has struggled to be a decent person all her life. And her options were never the same as the good girls in town. Growing up with a sick mother and limited resources, she does the best she can until a man she loves dies in a violent, intolerable situation where she blames herself. Then her world crumbles into drugs and self-hate. She's saved by the sound of a baby's cry, an unmanageable child who she bonds with and then needs as much as she wants his daddy.

Any luck Steven Corella has with the women in his life has been all bad. Sensitive, a man who works in a job unsuited to his inner nature, he manages to fool the world. When he finds he's to become a daddy, the tough-guy personality he's been portraying all along turns real. He hardens his heart and hides behind thick walls of protection he's carefully erected. And then Sunshine enters his world, and nothing makes sense anymore.

Chapter One

"Your man is one damn good-looker, Faith."

Laughing at the way her best friend's Aunt Barb strung together a compliment, Faith shook her head, depression settling in. "He's my boss, Barb. Not my man."

Unfortunately. The thought popped in, and as quickly she shut it down.

"You can't kid me, honey. When Sam greeted you by calling you Sunshine and swirled you in his arms, your guy's head swivelled like a hawk sighting prey. Until it seemed he recognized Sam, then he just looked confused."

Faith let the image play out in her head. "It was probably the name he didn't like. That's what the idiot at the casino called me when he tried to hire me for the night."

"Oh, you mean the idiot that Steven pounded the shit out of so that three bouncers had to pull him off – that idiot?" A grin played around the edges of Barb's smirk and her eyes twinkled.

"He'd learned my history in a shocking way, Barb. He'd thought of me as a normal woman who he'd just hired to be his precious baby's nanny. It would throw any man."

"You could be right, sweetie." Aunt Barb patted her cheek in a loving way. "Seems to me that if all he sees when he looks at you is his nanny, then he's not just stupid, he's blind, too." The older woman, dressed in a pantsuit that showed off her slim, medium height and colored blond hair, headed to the doorway and as Faith watched her leave, she saw both her friends, Cassi and Leni, leaning into the room. Both faces wore teasing grins.

Cassi entered first and headed for the champagne bottle, poured two drinks, added ginger ale to her own, then handed the girls their glasses.

A flowery whiff of perfume hovered around her, stronger than what one normally smelled as she walked by, but a scent Faith associated with her friend.

Cass's lovely wedding gown took up the biggest space in the smaller, old-fashioned kitchen. Soft ruffles of silk fluttered, rhinestones sewn into the material around her bare neck and shoulders glittered, and her black hair, with small roses woven throughout, shone in the overhead light.

As bridesmaids, Leni and Faith had chosen

similar dresses just not identical. Both wore long gowns in the same tone of stunning, baby-blue sparkling silk. But, Leni, her thick dark hair worn in draped curls over her shoulders had opted for a low-cut number that hugged her body, whereas blonde-haired Faith had gone conservative until she turned. The backless to her waist style suited her creamy pale skin. While the front lovingly hugged her chest, and swirled from her hips, it flared out with each step she took.

If her intention had been to downplay any hint of sexiness, she'd failed miserably. The material clung to her breasts, showing in detail their fullness and the swirling silkiness below the waist melded to her lush body every time she moved. Meanwhile, the gleaming softness of the skin on her back became an invitation to touch.

Since most of the guests were in the lit garden, hovering around the tent where masses of food kept them occupied, the girls had the room to themselves.

Cassi broke the silence and had their attention. "To us – three misfits who love each other!"

Leni lifted her goblet and added, "Sisters of the heart!" A clearing of Cassi's throat, made Leni chuckle as she added, "And half-sister to one weirdo who won't let the other forget."

Not to be outdone, Faith took it a step further as she contributed to the toast, "My adopted *sisters* who are both nutcases, but whom I adore and will always support."

Laughing, they all downed their drinks and then Leni dropped a bombshell. "Cass, you've been drinking non-alcoholic drinks yesterday and today. I bet you thought your sneaky maneuvering went unnoticed. Is there something you want to share with your sisters? Hmm?"

Cassi's blush had Faith reaching for her hand. "Oh my Lord, girlfriend, are you pregnant?" She waited, breath abated, praying that the news would be what they all wanted to hear.

"Shush. Don't breathe a word to anyone. I'm late. That's why I slipped out this morning. So I could buy some pregnancy tests just in case. On the off-chance that I could be, I'd never take any risks to harm Trace's baby."

Faith sighed, her smile huge. "It's your baby, too."

Leni exhaled, but with a slight groan thrown in, disgusted at their sappy, feminine expressions. "Oh, for heaven's sake, Cass, you mean to tell us you're hesitating. What? You afraid you're pregnant or you're not?"

Cassi put her arm around her bristling half-sister's shoulders. "Hold on, Leni. What I've seen between you and smitten Michael; you might be in need of a test too. I bought three so there'd be no doubt. You wanna use one?"

Laughing, Leni answered. "I'm too smart for that kind of shit. Ever heard of the pill?" Shaking off

Cassi's arm and turning the conversation back to the original subject, Leni grumbled. "Bet you intend to make us wait for the news."

"Yep. There'll only be two of us at the peeing ritual... or maybe three if it shows positive."

Laughing, Leni and Faith moved in for a group hug. Before Faith could escape, Cassi hit her with the question she'd been dreading. "Steven seems to be having a good time. He's been hanging out with Sam a lot."

Leni piped in, "Didn't think that would happen when Sam greeted you with your nickname, Sunshine, and that enthusiastic hug. I bet if Steven hadn't been carrying Raoul, he'd have made a fool of himself. The look on his face when he heard the nickname could freeze molasses."

Faith giggled. "You know why he reacted. He's so worried another slimeball will make a move on his nanny that we never go anywhere together except the grocery store and the mall.'

Bristling, Leni questioned. "You sayin' he's ashamed to be seen with you?"

"No, not ashamed as much as scared someone else will recognize me. Or at least that's what I believe."

Cassi put a calming hand on Leni's arm. "Back off, tiger. Remember Faith told us his casino manager's sick. No doubt, as the assistant, he's taken on all the extra work. Right now Vegas's crawling with tourists so it could be that he doesn't have the time to take her and Raoul out." Cassi turned to Faith. "Does he still come by and see the baby before he goes to sleep for the night?"

"Oh, sure. He's only missed once, and he phoned to apologize. They'd had a situation at work, some people passing out counterfeit bills or something."

Cassi held out both hands in a way that showed them she felt vindicated for supporting the man.

Facing Faith, Leni erupted, "Have you two had the talk, yet? The one where he's supposed to forgive you? Bastard." She held up her fist and pumped it in front of Faith. "I'd beg his forgiveness alright."

Laughing, Faith put both her hands against Leni's flushed cheeks. "You are my biggest fan, and I'd give you my best pair of Jimmy Choos if I had any. Truth is, ever since you overheard us saying we'd forgive each other that word has stuck in your craw. But... what you need to know is this. I do need his forgiveness or we can never move forward."

Cassi broke in. "That's just it, babe. Leni understands the same as I do. You've done nothing... NOTHING that requires his forgiveness. He has no right to judge your past. He either understands that life happens, lets go of the shit and moves on, or you leave him."

A tear snuck out before Faith could stop it. Her hands clasped together prayer-like, and the fear in her eyes wasn't faked. "That's just it. I could never leave him because that would mean I'd have to abandon Raoul. That baby is my lifeline to sanity and my path to a future. I'm clinging on as hard as I can, and if I have to take a little prejudice and judging then bring it on."

Leni bowed her head, her tone kind of joking. "I have an idea. Just get the prick to marry you and then make his life miserable."

Before they could stop giggling, the prick entered the kitchen with a squirming baby and a hard gleam in his eye. "Raoul woke up and misses you, Faith. And, Cassi, everyone is looking for you. It's something to do with your bouquet."

Chapter Two

Faith pondered the happiness that radiated inside her as she relaxed in the passenger seat of her boss's luxurious car. The streets of Vegas seemed surprisingly quiet but it was that time of dusk, the hour before darkness highlighted the dazzling bright lights of the city and the festivities of the crazy tourists letting loose began.

Steven appeared content behind the wheel, lost in his own thoughts, while Raoul, comfy in his baby seat, slept on the way home from Cassi's wedding.

As they often did, her thoughts reverted to the past. Cassi's twin brother had been the best thing that had ever happened to Faith. While they'd lived together, he'd treated her like a princess and she'd adored the man.

And even though he'd been killed in a mob shooting, a link had been forged between her and Cassi that could never be broken. A jewel, and not one to be taken lightly or for granted, Faith blessed the day that Raoul's twin sister came into her life.

If it hadn't been for Cassi's tenacity, they'd never have discovered the truth about the night Raoul had been murdered. She'd tracked down every person at the scene and eventually learned the truth – a truth that had shocked everyone.

No matter how many times they'd told her she wasn't responsible, a niggling guilt would plague Faith until her last breath. She'd unknowingly set up her dearest friend, Leni – who they eventually discovered to be Raoul and Cassi's half-sister – to be there at that moment of crisis, and therefore deeply involved.

She'd been forgiven by those who counted. Yet living with the fact that everything she'd done had been for the right reasons – to protect someone she loved – didn't make it better. The gnawing pain of missing her true love kept her awake in the black torturous hours of the night.

When she'd innocently suggested to Steven he might like to name his own baby Raoul, after he'd admitted to not having chosen anything for the newborn, she hadn't given any thought as to how that moniker would be a constant reminder in keeping her memories alive.

One of her better ideas? Maybe not. But she'd do it again knowing that her Raoul would have gotten a huge kick out of having the beautiful tiny boy as a namesake.

A snuffle from behind forced her attention back

to the moment, and she turned to check on baby Raoul. Played out from being fussed over by everyone at the crowded ceremony, exhaustion had caught up. He'd allowed their fawning as long as Faith stayed close, and he could keep her in his sight.

Dark hair, a cap around his small head, and dimples more noticeable every day, he still had the power to turn her heart to mush. Now at the end of his second month, he'd filled out and his big brown eyes, so like his daddy's, radiated glee plus a surprising bright-eyed intelligence.

The other wedding guests commented on this fact so it wasn't just her who saw his adorableness or his intellect. Faith grinned at her thoughts. Good Lord, she already had him graduating Harvard on the Dean's list.

Like any proud mama, she'd shown off Raoul, and her behavior had earned her a surprising gentle smile and half a hug from Steven, the baby's daddy. Standing next to the good-looker, as Aunt Barb described him, she'd swelled with pride to be among her friends, waiting for the bride to throw her bouquet.

When it landed smack dab in her arms, she'd grabbed the bunch to stop them from scaring Raoul and applause had thundered. Steven, like any man terrified of commitment, had leapt away, leaving her alone. Grinning, feeling stupidly excited while the baby tried munching on the rose petals, she gladly suffered her friends' congratulations and jovial teasing.

The moments before Cassi threw her bouquet stayed with her. When he'd stepped close and put his arm around her back. His surprising tenderness had lightened her heart and made her wonder if they might have a chance to heal the breech that had festered and grown.

Since the day he'd found out the truth about her previous lifestyle as a hooker in a sleazy nightclub, he'd kept a distance between them as wide as the Mississippi.

Settling back into her comfy position, she relived the night before when all three girls had stayed at Cassi's house and celebrated the upcoming nuptials together. For her and Leni, it was their version of guard duty. To keep Trace away from his bride-to-be and to hinder their friend from freaking out from last-minute jitters. The reality would be more like Cassi sneaking out to be with her fiancé.

Their last night where all three girls were still single and could act like crazies without feeling the pressure that married women should behave with more decorum, they'd cut loose.

Dancing, drinking fancy drinks – Cass making her and Leni their favorite margaritas while she drank some concoction that looked like champagne with fruit – they'd acted insane, giggling, weeping over lost loved ones, telling stories of their younger years and bonding even closer than they'd done so far.

They'd sworn to carry on the ritual of "chick's night" once a month no matter what was happening in their lives. Then in the wee hours of the morning, they'd all passed out on the same bed.

It wasn't until the doorbell rang that she'd jerked awake; her thoughts instantly flying to her small charge. Maybe a screaming baby had registered in her mind before she'd actually reached consciousness. Once she'd accepted it wasn't a dream, she'd known that Raoul needed her and therefore his daddy, Steven, needed her too.

When she'd opened the door to the sheepish man, who hadn't had the benefit of a shower, a hair brush or a shave, she'd grinned and reached for Raoul.

"I'm sorry, Faith. After you settled him last time, he stayed sleeping until a couple of hours ago. Since then, he's worked himself into a rage."

Quickly, Steven had passed her charge over to her arms, and she'd admonished the child in her gentle way. "Shush, munchkin. You'll wake up the whole neighborhood." He responded as usual, and the loud crying ceased, turning into a peevish wail and then to a complaining grumble.

Steven's words still reverberated and brought a smile. "Bless you, honey. And I mean that from the bottom of my heart."

Rather than the small baby tote she normally

used, he'd leaned over to put down a large black bag he probably used himself for overnight trips. Stacked brimful with way too much gear, he'd been forced to leave it open. "I didn't know what to bring so I gathered up what you had near his crib. I added his bottles and formula and—"

Laughing, unable to help herself, she'd nodded. "Looks like you've packed his whole bedroom."

Head lowered to hide the blush, his hands on his hips, he took a step back. "Look, if you need anything I've forgotten, just text me. I'll run it over. I have to stop at the casino later, but I'll be back here in time for the wedding."

For just a second, she'd thought he'd intended to cancel, and her heart had sunk. Now, she wanted to swing the still fretful baby around the veranda in a dance of happiness.

"Oh, good! I'm glad you decided to come. I know Cassi and Trace will be happy, too. They haven't had a chance to really meet you, and yet they've invited us out so many times."

"Sorry," said the man who looked anything but. "As I explained before, when the floor manager was in the hospital, all the casino responsibilities fell on my shoulders. You know how hectic it's been. Now that he's better, I'll have more freedom."

"Good. Raoul loves his time with you." She'd bowed her head so he couldn't see the truth. She looked forward to his visits as well. Putting it down to spending too many hours on her own with just a baby for company, she backed away from the niggling suspicion that his presence made her tingle, feel alive... even happy.

As he made his way back to the car, she'd noticed his pajama bottoms peeking out from his pant legs not quite hiding his bare feet in his dress shoes. It appeared that Steven had been in a hurry to bring her his son. She couldn't help but let the pride glow as she kissed her little buddy. "That's my boy. You remind your daddy how important I am."

Once inside, an excited Cassi spied her bundle and came forward with her arms waiting. "Raoul! I love this little twerp, even if his lungs outdo Pavarotti's." Faith passed him over and carried the load of gear into the bedroom. Cassi followed, kissing his small cheeks and nuzzling him in a way he seemed to enjoy. "He's adorable."

Bizarrely, Raoul, appearing to understand Cassi's words, blessed her with his most endearing grin and threw in a gurgle that sounded very close to affirmation.

***

Shaking off her nostalgia, Faith glanced over at the man's relaxed body behind the steering wheel. She recognized the quirky smile he often wore when snuggling Raoul, holding him prone on his thigh and having the goofy conversation parents tend to have with small babies.

She loved watching him perform when he came

for his nightly visits. Those moments were the highlight of her day, and she always made sure Raoul had been bathed and that he'd napped earlier so he'd be in a good mood.

Strangely, she also made sure she looked her best. Intending on cutting off her long hair, she'd backed off when he'd made a comment about how the sun turned it golden. Instead, she'd had Cassi take her to her own hairdresser, and the young stylist had shaped it instead.

Feathered around her cheeks, it brought out the various blue tones of her eyes and gave her heart-shaped face a frame that gained a lot of attention if the many male looks were to be counted.

According to Cassi's comment when they left the shop, one she had trouble believing, "Goodness, Faith. You were beautiful before but with your hair so sleekly modern now, you're stunning."

Unsure why, that comment had thrown her into a spin. Instead of leaving it down, she tended to curl the mass in a clip off her face rather than let her boss see it fixed up.

Except for today.

When she'd appeared all dressed up, hair gleaming, ready for her special day, he'd flinched and turned away. But not before admiration flared, which he'd quickly hidden behind his shuttered eyes.

It had taken a lot of convincing to get Steven to

even come with her to the wedding. Most likely, he'd agreed because he knew he'd be left in charge of the baby for the whole day. And he'd already suffered from babysitting a cranky Raoul the night before.

Even though, before she'd left, she'd put Raoul down for the night, he'd woken after midnight, and Steven had had to call her so she could talk the baby down. Once Raoul heard her voice – Steven kept the phone on speaker – he'd drifted off. When Steven had surprised her with Raoul that morning, she'd known he'd panicked.

Poor man still suffered from the last experience when he'd kicked her out after learning of her history. He'd stayed with newborn Raoul alone. Within a day, he'd fetched her from Leni's aunt's house.

He'd caved like an alcoholic faced with a bottle of whiskey over his principles of hiring a bad girl versus his son's happiness.

Happy that he'd seen the light – only learning a long time later that he'd had a visit from her two convincing friends, Cassi and Leni – she'd returned to the apartment to resume her nanny duties, expecting that they'd soon talk and clear the air.

He'd said they would.

She'd agreed.

Except... that hadn't happened.

She hoped he'd be approachable when she

broached the subject, but it hadn't transpired in quite that way. All he'd said were the words, "I forgive you. Now let's put it behind us and move on."

Though she'd prayed they'd be able to discuss her previous lifestyle where everything got laid out on the table, his unmoving tone had scared her into nodding and letting it go.

One day she'd force the issue... but not yet. Not until she felt better about herself and had more confidence in her position. Then she'd approach him and ask that they discuss his concerns about her previous employment as Sunshine... a hooker at the notorious Lipstick Club in the city of sin.

Chapter
Three

Steven drove into the underground parking of the apartment building where he paid the rent for a small suite, home for Raoul and Faith. Guilt struck as he pulled into their slot.

He'd intended to rent a vehicle for Faith so she could take Raoul for outings, yet weeks had passed and he'd done nothing.

Sure, he had good reasons for putting things off, he'd been working like a guy trying to prove something ever since his boss had gotten laid up, but that had to end now. He needed to get his life back in order and to stop living on the edge.

Ever since he'd found himself by the hospital bassinet, watching his screaming newborn and dreading the moment he'd be forced to take on his care, life had started spinning.

Chasing after Natalie, the baby's mother, had been a joke. The bitch had meant every word she'd said after Raoul's birth. *"I don't want no baby. I never signed up to be a mommy when we met. Yet I gave you nine stinking months of my life to give the kid a decent start. Just get your lawyer to send me the check and whatever papers I need to sign, and he's all yours."*

Shaking off the memory, Steven reached into the back seat to unlock the straps holding his little man safely in the baby seat. He carefully lifted him out so he could pass him to Faith's extended arms.

"If you take the monster, I'll get the bag."

"Don't forget my flowers."

He grinned. "I won't." He still couldn't get over the joy his babysitter had displayed when she'd caught the bouquet of roses. He'd seen women light up over jackpots totaling thousands of dollars, and none had outshone her.

He fetched the black case full of baby gear that had made her smile earlier at his sudden feeling of discomfort. Chuckling to himself, he realized why she'd had that reaction. In his haste, he hadn't really noticed the amount of paraphernalia he'd stuffed together in his panic.

Hell, he'd brought enough for ten babies. He shook his head, dropped his load and leaned against the car. Faith had disappeared into the elevator, no doubt wanting to get Raoul into bed without waking him up, so he had a few moments to catch his breath.

All the way home, he'd been reliving the afternoon, not wanting to admit the real reason he'd passed on every invitation she'd shyly shared for them to spend time with her friends. He'd refused them all.

Sure, he'd been busy at work. That excuse hadn't been a lie. Only, he could have made the time if he'd really wanted it to happen. Thing was – he didn't. He'd wanted to completely sever ties for both of them with anyone in her past.

Ashamed, he admitted dreading having to handle any derision she might have to face from her past, any slurs or bad manners her so-called friends might have shown. Of course, that hadn't happened. Both of them had been treated like royalty and Faith had been shown only loving kindness and gentle caring.

And it wasn't only the women. A man he had the utmost respect for, a lawman he'd had the good fortune to have worked within an undercover operation where a bunch of counterfeit bills had shown up in the casino, had been there.

Agent Sam Smith had solved the case, arrested the offenders and arranged it so slyly that not even a ripple had passed through the other gamblers enjoying their evening.

His admiration for Sam and his men's acuity in handling the crisis had left Steven and his manager blessing the agents and breathing a sigh of relief that it had been handled so professionally.

To see the same agent cuddling Faith, his friendly overtures met with her own gushing,

"Sam. It's wonderful to see you again," had Steven taking a step back and looking at his own behavior. Even Sam calling her Sunshine hadn't sounded like a slur, more a title of affection.

At first, he'd watched carefully, bristling, waiting to attack anyone who disrespected the woman he trusted to look after his most precious possession. Only it never happened. Instead, all her friends were protective of her too.

By their actions, they let him know he'd better treat her right. From their fondness, they taught him she was cared about, precious to all who were there and if anyone had to prove their worthiness, it sure as hell wasn't the hooker.

It was him.

Talk about a wake-up call. It was like someone had stuck a fuse under his ass, lit it and made him see how his own actions were small-minded and sad. After all, what gave him the right to judge the woman? The person who had saved his sanity and became a mother for his deserted son deserved better.

Remembering back to the day he'd first seen her in the hospital, a blonde angel cuddling his surprisingly happy baby. His heart had flown right out of his chest, gathered the two of them together and then closed the door up tight after they were safe inside.

From then on, he'd lived within that bubble of tenderness and delight. Once she'd promised to work for him, dreams had begun to form. They would learn about each other, start a romance and eventually unite to build a happy home.

As he'd expected, her letters of recommendation had been well-written and glowing. Based on the information he'd read, he quickly reaffirmed his offer for the job and hurried her to the apartment where he'd previously set up Natalie while she'd awaited the baby's birth.

Though he lived at the Casino in the assistant manager's suite, he'd still had this place redone before she'd moved in. He'd had his secretary order different furniture and had it professionally cleaned for her and Raoul. Nothing was too good for his son and his new nanny.

Remembering now how he'd drifted through those happy days. When he'd believed her to be the angel he saw whenever he looked her way. It only followed that he'd relive the thud of his heart hitting cement when faced with the truth.

His angel had been nothing but a slut who'd worked in one of the most notorious clubs in the city. Imagine how many men had known her body? How many sickos had used her? And she'd allowed it to happen, taken money for her collaboration.

No matter how many times those images formed, when he'd let his mind travel into that black sickness of jealousy and pain, misery consumed him. It ate away at his clear-headedness. Killer instincts, he never knew he possessed, overwhelmed. Raising his hands, he covered his face.

Fierce emotions formed fists that dug into his eye sockets. Unexpected tears spilled through shaking fingers and his body quivered. What was a man to do? How could he delete visions that drove him insane?

This had to stop. He had to work through it, especially after today. Which way was forward – learning trust and maybe building a future?

Sighs wracked his body. He gritted his teeth and wiped his face, swallowing the rage that appeared every time he let his thoughts go to the dark side.

Forgiveness!

He needed to forgive her.

But how?

Chapter Four

Faith, still reeling from Steven's abrupt departure after delivering the baby's things and her beautiful flowers, quickly sought a jar big enough for the sweet-smelling bouquet.

For the hundredth time, she buried her face amongst the roses to inhale their strong scent. She wished she could have a garden of her own so she could grow these beauties. When she looked at the vivid pink of the petals, and let herself delve deep into nature's construction, she marveled at their perfection and beauty.

Opening every cupboard, she could find nothing to use as a vase. Not even a milk carton she'd made do with in her past for the one and only time she'd ever gotten flowers.

Thinking back, she remembered how Leni had bribed her cousin, Mani, to give her Faith's address. She'd delivered yellow roses as a thank you for saving her from being raped at the upstairs parlor of the club.

That night, Leni had been there solely to deliver papers to their boss. But she'd stumbled into the room where the working girls gave lap dances, shared drugs and led the clients to smaller chambers so they'd spend more for special favors.

After Faith had said goodbye to her own client, she'd entered the salon to see an ugly bruiser attacking a girl she knew didn't work there. Moving in, she'd lured the idiot away from poor shaking Leni. It had taken very little for the asshole to turn to someone willing rather than having to force his unwanted attentions on the terrified girl who'd only fought him off.

As a way to express her gratitude, Leni had shown up at Faith's apartment with yellow roses and her hand out in friendship. Turns out, the beating Faith had taken from the prick had been worth it. Leni had become her first real female friend, a priceless gift she'd be thankful for all the days of her life.

Reliving the past had her clenching the stems too tightly and a thorn's puncture brought her back to reality. There was nowhere she could put the beauties safely. If she wanted to carry them with her, to display in every room, she needed a vase.

Marie! Yes. The girl in the apartment across from hers had been friendly. In dire straits, she'd knocked on Faith's door yesterday morning, begging coffee. And they'd visited in the hallway a number of times. She'd fallen for Raoul's goos and grins, making a fuss over the little guy, and that behavior had won Faith over.

Instinctively, Faith knew she'd lend her a vase if she had one. Happy now, she immersed the flowers in the sink rather than leaving them on the counter, and filled it halfway with water.

She checked to make sure that Raoul was sleeping and snatched up the small baby monitor. Leaving the door open, she stepped across the hall and knocked on the door.

Music or maybe the loudness from the television revealed Marie was home. When the door flung open and a male face appeared, Faith was shocked. Expecting the other woman, her smile slid and she stepped back.

The man had obviously been drinking booze or bathing in the stuff, because the fumes from his body and rank breath could drop a horse. Finding a strange woman at his door, he seemed equally stunned. But he was the first to recover.

"Yeah?"

Though intimidated, Faith stood her ground. "Is Marie home?" She watched as his expression underwent a change and recognition took over.

At that moment, images of being brutalized flooded her, and she remembered.

Oh, no! No, please God, no! This man had been one

of her regulars after Raoul had died. He'd demanded she take care of his needs, because when she'd lived in that fog of drugs and indifference, she'd never cared what happened to her. Relishing pain as punishment for her sins, he'd happily accommodated her, inflicting beatings every time he'd visited. Being confronted by him here, every hope she'd built for a future with Steven shriveled, crumbled and died.

"What do you want? Hold it. I know who you are. Sunshine – my favorite. You've changed your hair. But I'd know that sexy body of yours anywhere. So, why are you here, babydoll?"

Turning away, Faith mumbled, "Nothing important. I hoped Marie could lend me a vase for some flowers."

"She's gone to visit her mom. But I can give you a vase, Sunshine. In fact, I'd be happy to help you out for a small favor in return. If I remember correctly, you made me a very happy man until you disappeared from the club. I kept asking for you, but they said you'd left. Now I see why. You've set yourself up in your own apartment." His sneer became uglier with glee. "I can't tell you how pleased I am to find you living right next door. Like, it's totally convenient, baby." His arm shot out and he hauled her in close. His stink and aggressive actions ramped up her fear. She struggled, which only made him chuckle and tighten his hold.

"Let me go. I'm not doing that anymore." She

got her arms between them and pushed against his chest. "Back off and leave me alone."

Fogged with lust and alcohol, the creep never hesitated, never slowed down his attack. Fantasies overcoming his stunted brain cells, he grunted his joy while pushing her against the wall and mashing his hardened groin against her tender body.

"See how hot you make me, Bitch? Am I gonna give it to you tonight. It'll be worth every penny. I need some lovin' and you're just the girl I want."

"No! Stop. You're hurting me." Words had no effect on the loser. Faith knew it was just a matter of a few seconds before he dragged her inside his apartment and raped her.

In Raoul's male demanding voice, instructions suddenly beat inside her head. *If a mean prick attacks, ring the bell I gave you. If you can't get to it, use your mouth and bite hard. Then follow it up with your knee*. Obeying his instructions, she ground her teeth into the closest arm. He screamed and let her go. Effective, more than she'd anticipated, she quickly kneed him in the groin and pushed on his lowered head with all her might.

The results were amazing. He landed back in his apartment crumpled on the floor, clutching his privates and squealing like a baby. Now free, she twirled back inside her own place and slammed the door.

First, she locked it and then she latched the chain. Shaking, sobbing, her legs too weak to hold her upright, she slunk to the floor in a pool of blue silk and lay in a fetal position. Rocking back and forth, sobs tearing her apart, her thoughts turned nasty from fear and pain.

Good Lord, why would you do this to me now, just when things were beginning to turn in my favor? That man's a monster, and he lives next door. Why do you hate for me to be happy?

Lying there, feeling sick, Faith's mind traveled to Marie and what the pretty girl had shared in their quick chats. She'd mentioned a fiancé but from the way she'd talked about him, Faith had gotten the impression the man walked on water. If the scum who'd just attacked her was that man, then her neighbor either had to be delusional or he deserved an Academy Award.

Truth of the matter, many of the men who'd paid for favors in their club had families, worked hard and lived a normal everyday existence. They just craved some spice in their lives to keep them going. A night out with the boys, some cool drugs, a girl – or two – and they'd go home to mama with no one the wiser and behave until the next go-round.

She didn't judge these guys. With her background, she'd never felt she had the right to condemn anyone else. But a woman beater didn't deserve loyalty or consideration. Besides, she knew she hadn't seen the last of him. Not if the curses he'd spewed before she'd closed her door were any indication.

He'd be wanting revenge.

Chapter Five

The phone!

Her chiming ringtone hauled her back from the dark side. Despair had overtaken all her senses as her thoughts twirled, caged hopelessness oozing in. She swiped at the mess of tears on her face and checked the caller ID. It was Steven.

Shit!

Shaky, scared, stomach clenched, her pulse rioting, she doubted if she'd make any sense. But he'd be frantic if she didn't answer his call.

Swallowing the fresh tears that welled up, she groaned to clear her voice, took a deep breath and spoke, "Hel-lo."

"Hello? Are you okay, Faith? You sound far away."

Get it together. "Oh, sorry. I had my hand over the speaker. I didn't want to wake up Raoul."

"Were you with him? Sorry. I had to speak to you, but I never know when you're in his room. I just wanted to apologize for leaving you so abruptly earlier. Something came up, and I needed to get back to the casino."

Voice low but steadier, she coughed and then answered. "Don't worry, Steven. Is everything okay there?"

He hesitated before admitting they'd restored peace. "Just some overeager gamblers who think they can cheat the system. You know the old saying 'the house always wins'. Well in this case, it turned out to be true and some fellows had a hard time accepting their loss."

Grounded by his voice, she wanted to keep him on the line. He made her feel safe. "I feel sorry for people who get caught up in the hype, who depend on winning. It does happen. But more times it doesn't."

"A hell of a lot more times. Did Raoul give you a hard time after I left?"

"Of course not, he's still sleeping. I think everyone wore him out today."

"You've got great friends, Faith. They treated us like family, and I appreciated it. Next time Cassi and Trace want to get together, I'll make time, I promise." Softened, husky tones soothing, his voice mesmerized. "Oh, oh. Gotta go. See you tomorrow. I'll come over after lunch and take you shopping."

Oh, no. What if jerk-off next door sees us leaving? What if he says something in front of Steven?

"I really don't need anything at the store, Steven.

Please don't worry."

"Hey, it's a pleasure not a chore, honey. See you around one."

Honey!

It was the second time today he'd used a pet name; she liked it. But she didn't deserve it. How could she be anyone's honey when others saw her exactly the way she was. As a street-walking slut who hated looking in the mirror.

A memory jiggled, pulling her to the present. She began to panic. Where was Raoul's baby monitor? Oh God! She must have dropped it during their struggle in the hallway.

Energized, adrenalin pulsing, she ran to the entrance but stopped before she unlocked the door.

What if he was waiting for her to come out? She checked the peephole, and surveyed the space. Empty. She slowly eased the door open but the floor was empty. He must have picked up her monitor.

In a panic, she shut the door and relocked herself inside.

Bastard! He took it.

Shoulders slumped; she tiptoed into Raoul's bedroom and scooped up the sleeping child. Then she carried him into her room and sunk onto the bed beside him. Curling her body around him protectively, she lay there while ideas rampaged only to be dropped as another shot into place.

Raoul's grumbling woke her from the nightmare a few hours later. She'd been chased by a monster with her neighbor's face and the body of a beast. No matter where she hid, he found her by listening to a monitor that recorded her breathing. There was no escape. None...

Raoul settled down as soon as he heard her voice and felt her arms. The baby had learned how to charm, and he used his wiles all the time she changed and fed him. His beautiful deep pools of soft brown followed her every move. Gurgling happily once full, he babbled his thoughts the way babies liked to do as long as they had your complete attention.

For Faith, talking to Raoul had become her favorite part of his baby care. He listened, eyes following her expression. If she laughed, he grinned. If she whispered soft words of adoration, he preened. Within minutes, he took over the conversation and shared his own stories. Of course, there was no sense to his utterances. But there was a cadence to the sounds he made, and she loved listening.

He repaid her attention by telling her stories in baby babble and bestowing on her his utmost charm. She adored the child, loved him past words. None that could describe her feelings. She'd die for him. And any threat to him made her wild.

"No one will ever hurt you, Baby boy." She caressed his plump cheek and kissed his head.

Scooping him closer, her arms wrapped around his wiggling little body, she released the fear that suddenly reappeared. "I'd kill him first."

Chapter Six

Anticipating the coming visit to see his son, Steven dressed in casual clothes. He chose blue jeans and his favorite light green shirt that showed off his upper physique and didn't have to be tucked in.

Leaning forward, he surveyed his appearance and zoomed in on his face. He'd always hated his eyes, his father's eyes, dark brown daggers of dislike and inebriated anger. He picked out clothes on purpose that might lighten them from black marble.

In high school, one of his girlfriends had commented that the tones changed depending on what he wore and so he dressed carefully, always aware of colors he knew would work a little magic.

His dad, a man he'd had no respect for, Steven often wished he'd taken after his Irish mother in looks as well as personality. She'd been his best fan, his main support and his loving friend for the years she lived. Steven, being her only child, had been lucky. She'd passed on her love of life, her sensitive nature, her brains and her spirit.

When he'd turned seven, she'd been the force that had finally driven his old man from their lives. A hard drinker his dad, lazy, never taking responsibility for anything, years later she'd told Steven – Stevie as she'd called him – *I didn't want you influenced by that man. He might have given you his genes, but I'd be damned if I was going to allow him to teach you his rotten habits.*

"What attracted you to him in the first place, Mom? Why ever did you marry him?" Steven had wondered what his sweet, lovely mom had ever seen in the hard-assed complainer.

"You never met the Fergus I knew from years ago. That man could charm a bird to eat crumbs from his hand."

"And you were that bird."

"Yes. I was his bird, dazzled by his charming ways. But I soon realized the hand was empty and it could hurt."

"Aw, mom. I wished I'd been old enough to know what went on. I'da stopped him."

"It wasn't your battle to fight, Stevie. One day, you'll love someone, and you'll need to be there for them. Then it'll be your turn. This time was my turn. I made the decision that you came first. You needed to grow up free from seeing the destruction a cowardly bastard could reap, even if his lying lips could woo and those deep browns could ensnare.

We're both well rid of the man."

Shaking off the gloom memories of his father usually triggered, he pictured his red-haired mom and a smile travelled throughout his body to reach his lips. A tiger for her boy, she'd fought his battles, teaching him along the way how to win his own. She'd have loved his little Raoul.

Saddened that he'd lost her to breast cancer a few years earlier, he compared Raoul's nanny to her – something he'd done with every woman he'd met over the years. While Raoul's real mother shared the same passion for excitement, his mother would have loathed her unconscionable decision to leave her child and take the money.

Recognition appeared suddenly and he believed, without any doubt, that she would have liked Faith. Their similarities – Faith's sweet nature and love for Raoul, would have won her instance approval.

Until mom learned the truth about her past.

A Christian woman, church-going until the day she'd died, his perfect mom would have judged the beautiful girl and found her immoral. But then, he wasn't his mother. She'd made her mistakes.

If he was about to make some of his own, then so be it.

***

Shaking off his reminiscing, he grabbed his keys, his wallet and used the staff elevator to get to the underground employee's concrete parking lot.

Feeling on top of the world, having come to a decision over his reflections earlier, he'd decided to accept Faith's past and ignore her earlier life – to forgive her.

Feeling magnanimous, revelling in his choice to be a better man than many he knew who would walk away without a qualm, he hummed along with the song on the radio.

Hot sun greeted him, spurring him into searching for his sunglasses. Driving along the boulevard, he let his gaze shuffle to the tourists having the time of their lives.

It never failed to lift his spirits when he saw couples, hand in hand, dressed in their vacation garb and enjoying themselves. Groups wandering, laughing, sharing, heading to certain fun-filled activities, looking happy to be alive and in the Fun City he loved.

Arriving at the apartment, he bounded up the stairs rather than taking the elevator and saw a man knocking on Faith's door. The guy appeared to be upset. His knocks turned to fist slams and his voice rang with disgust.

"What's up, man?" Steven stepped forward, ready for a confrontation.

"What's it to you?" The prick had an attitude, one that instantly offended, ruffling his earlier great mood.

"You're banging on *my* door. What do you want?" Steven adopted the same authoritative tone he used when dealing with assholes at the casino.

"What do you mean your door? A woman lives here."

"So. Why are you bothering her?"

"I have something of hers, she dropped it in the hallway. I wanted to return it. Jesus, what is this, an inquisition? Tell her I'll bring it over later." The asshole's demeanour suddenly switched. "Have your fun but leave some for me."

Before Steven could make heads or tails of what the bastard meant, he swivelled off to catch the elevator. *What a weirdo! I'll warn Faith to watch out for him.*

With his mind still on the idiot, he slid his key into the lock and twisted the door handle. He came to a dead stop when a chain across the opening tightened and held. *What the hell?*

"Faith, it's me." From the corner of his eye, he saw the material of her dress flared on the floor. *Jesus!* "Faith, are you okay? Did you fall? Open the door."

Sudden movement, her dress disappeared and seconds later she unlocked the bolt. "I'm sorry, Steven. I dropped my ahh... earring in the corner."

Relief rioted. The strangeness of the past few minutes fled, and his sense of tension faded. He followed her to the living room. "Oh good, you found it." He lifted his hand toward her ear.

Shocked at her flinching reaction, he stepped back. That's when he noticed her paleness. The colorless lips even with her pretty pink lipstick applied. Waves of stress surrounded her body though she tried to hide her tension.

Suddenly it clicked. "Was that fellow bothering you?"

Stiffness appeared – in her shoulders and back especially. Her gaze slid away as did her welcoming smile.

"Faith. When I came in, there was a neighbour using his fist on the door and you didn't hear him?"

She whipped around to face him. "I heard him already." Her voice rose, bordering on hysteria. "I don't want anything to do with that man. Some creeps seem to think that a woman living alone is fair prey, and I-I won't have it."

Shocked by the suddenness of her attack, he stepped back. "Fine. Calm down, honey. Do you want me to have a little talk with him?"

"No. I want you to ignore him. I will too, and once Maria returns from her mother's, he'll behave."

"Maria?"

"That's his fiancé."

"Bastard is trying to mess with you while his lady is away?" His voice turned to concrete. "I see him hanging around again, he's going to hear about it." Bone-shuddering rage shocked Steven into growling his words. The jealous reaction caught him off-guard.

What caught him even more off-guard was her

comeback. "You're going to say nothing. Do you hear me?" Her finger pointed at him, coming close to drilling his chest. "Don't talk to him or pay attention to that vile *worm*. I-I don't want to upset Maria. I like her."

Shocked at the suddenness of her attack, he backed off but his mind had been made up. They would have a chat. "Fine, but I better not see him at our door again or he's going to learn a lesson he won't soon forget."

***

Raoul's sudden screams caught them off-guard. Both turned in the direction of the bedroom with Steven in the lead. "Hey tiger, daddy's here. Don't cry." He picked up the baby and seemed shocked when the screams changed to the normal grumbling of a baby with needs.

He didn't see what Faith did, Raoul's eyes searching for her. Once his eyes made contact, he settled down, the volume of his crying lessoning dramatically.

"Faith, did you see that? He's happy to see me. When I picked him up, he stopped crying. That's the first time he's ever done that."

Not able to help herself, she chuckled while nodding. "Why don't you let me change him for you, and then you can feed him his bottle. Would you like to?"

"Do you think he'll take the milk from me?"

"Of course he will, won't you munchkin."

Tickling Raoul under his chin and getting a gurgling response of good cheer, she laughed. "Here let me wash him and put a clean diaper on his royal highness. He gets very righteously irate when his pants are wet."

Steven watched her every move, his body so close that her skin tingled in reaction. Offering his finger for the baby to hold on to put his chest in contact with her back and her body's response weakened her knees.

Heart beating like a tom-tom, this time stirred by soft feelings rather than fear, Faith took her time changing the little man on purpose. Raoul's big-eyed grin in reaction to Steven's cooing in a manner that a large, deep-voiced, masculine guy would do, opened her eyes to the ways a regular man might act as a daddy.

Mushy now, her heart softened like never before, she stepped back without thinking and felt arms close around her in a hug. She didn't move. Anticipation that had been formed from her experiences of most men, she held her breath and waited for him to grab, hurt, demand.

Instead, she felt his hands rub her arms tenderly as he leaned in and nuzzled her neck.

"You always smell wonderful, like flowers and sunshine."

Oh, God!

She wrenched herself from his arms and made her way to the door. "I'll get the bottle heated."

Chapter
Seven

You idiot! She'd been willing, responsive, loving and he'd said the one word guaranteed to upset her. Clenching his hands before reaching for both hips, head lowered to stare at nothing; he decided that it had to stop. An innocent remark where he'd spoken her nickname shouldn't be allowed to wreck such a sweet moment.

Raoul suddenly began a monologue of baby talk and Steven could swear he was giving him hell. "You're right, buddy. I am a nincompoop. Soon as we come back from the mall, I'm straightening this out. Tell her I forgive her and we'll move on. Sound like a plan?"

Shocked at Raoul's reaction, Steven swore later that his son had looked disgusted with him before he let out a bellow. She'd been out of his sight too long.

He scooped up the sudden red-faced screamer

and headed for where he knew she'd be. Shocked to see her hunched over, arms around her middle, appearing like an inner pain had been too much for her to bear, he cautiously called to her, "Faith, honey, Raoul missed you."

She whipped around, reaching. "Oh my, I'm sorry your majesty. What was I thinking? You're a hungry bear and my head's in the clouds." She gave her charge a sweet cuddle, nuzzling his tiny neck with her lips and the crying stopped. Grasping the bottle from the warming pan, she headed for the sofa in the other room and stood in front, waiting for Steven to take his seat.

Frazzled after the earlier tension, he hesitated. "Are you sure he'll let me?"

"This bambino is starving, trust me. He'll be happy to have his bottle, and I'll stay close by to make sure he behaves."

Within a few seconds, Steven held Raoul in his arms and watched his beautiful baby take nourishment. This routine never failed to create a rush of contentment.

Filled with intense love, his chest close to exploding, incredulity crept in. How could he have helped create such perfection? The tiny face, so like his own, guaranteed the child was his son. Eyes, replicas, sussed him out before closing in rapture from the enjoyment of his formula. Sudden tears welled and he fought to stop them from unmanning him in front of the sweet girl, leaning close.

She moved to gently clear away milk that Raoul dribbled, and her face came within inches. Unthinking, he looked at her and knew she saw his emotion.

Knew it when she reached out and searched for his hand. And when she smiled tenderly and nudged her shoulder against his.

Why Faith seeing his tears didn't bother him, he decided he'd assess later. All he knew was at that tender moment, he didn't mind at all. When her own eyes filled, he instinctively leaned toward her until her forehead met his.

They touched. Their eyes met and held. Never in his life had he experienced such an overpowering sense of warmth. Affection blossomed until everything surrounding them faded. Only Faith! Her pools of blueness, her beautiful face... her sweet tenderness.

He carefully set his satisfied sleeping bundle safely on the other end of the sofa and then pulled Faith over to sit on his knee. Scared she'd fight him, he didn't relax until he felt her warm body slide into his arms.

Without a word spoken, he nuzzled her neck and let his hands caress her face; lifting her soft hair away from the spot where he most wanted his lips to start their search to her mouth.

Totally engrossed, he kissed his way along her arched throat and up her chin to willing, warm lips.

When they touched, an explosion occurred and left him trembling. Never before had a kiss tasted so good or had such a strong reaction on him. Yearning, passion, whatever the romantics call it left him weak and wanting more... a lot more.

Her low sigh became a moan of interest, signalling her acceptance. Her body snuggled closer. She gave more in one kiss than any female he'd ever met, and the riveting heat doubled.

In seconds, their combined breathing turned intense. Sensations and urges overtook good judgment until entering her soft body and sharing his passion became his only goal.

***

Faith's head swam and her senses recognized a difference. She'd had men's hands all over her body but they'd never taken her to these heights before. Ever!

They'd used her body, but they'd never broken through that barrier where she cared, wanted... loved. Not until Raoul. And never like this.

Once his hands travelled to her breasts, she delighted in her confidence. They would please him. Without a doubt. She'd been told before – often.

His pleasure mattered, and when he finally had his lips around her nipples and his warm hands caressing her back, shoulders and opposite breast, she let him pleasure her to his heart's content.

In turn, she took advantage of the moment to

indulge her own desires. Almost since the beginning, his body had tantalized hers.

She'd fantasized about petting him, having her hands on him. Knowing all the tricks of making a man happy, deeper ecstasy was only a few tricks of foreplay. But she let him lead the way and joyfully went along with his needs.

When he began stroking her legs and working his way to the ultimate soaking wet goal between them, she shifted her weight to give him full access.

She undid his belt, his pants and reached inside to fondle his hardness. Pleased with the size, shape and length she held gently in her hand, she shuddered, writhing in anticipation. Dizzy with desire, hot and wild, needing him inside her heavy, soaked entrance, she finally called to him.

"Steven."

"Honey, Faith, you're so beautiful... so soft. Let me. Please darling. Show me."

"God, Steven. Yes. Please."

Overcome with yearning and spurred on by his words, she moved to straddle him, squirming, shuddering, letting him know she was ready. With the top of her sundress around her waist and her skirt pushed up, her soaked thong was all that stood in the way of their joining.

That lasted only as long as the threads held from his frantic yank and within seconds he had reached his goal and they were in heaven.

***

My God! He'd never exploded like that before. He'd felt as if he'd die if he hadn't been able to make love to her, be inside her, pleasure her. And from the sounds he'd heard, she'd been in the same heaven he'd found for himself. Intensely gratified, spasms still rippling, he held her sweating body close and sifted his shaking hands through her hair.

He felt her lips kiss his chest more than once and knew no man had ever been loved with more passion or more intensely than what he'd just experienced. Peace and contentment began to glide over him. A snuffling noise came from the baby a few feet away.

His son.

Faith and his son.

How had he won such a jackpot, been such a winner?

There was still one thing standing between them and a future. He knew it. And he knew who held the reins. Tolerance for her past would clear away any hurdles still between them. The discussion would let them move forward.

Him, Raoul and Faith together... a family.

Suddenly, a cry heralded the baby waking up. Increasing in volume, Raoul began to inform them he meant business. He wanted his nanny and Steven had to share.

Loath to release her luscious warmth, he had no choice. She kissed him one last time, stood to fix her clothes and picked up Raoul to take him to his room for a change.

Opportunity lost; he decided they'd have this discussion at the next available opportunity later that evening. Once he said what he knew she wanted most to hear, he'd prove again with his body how much she'd come to mean to him. He'd say the three important words he'd bit back this time. Then she'd never have reason to question his commitment.

He'd man up.

He'd forgive her.

Chapter
Eight

"You forgive me? You ass! I never asked for your forgiveness. According to people who love me, I don't *need* your forgiveness." Crying so hard she could barely say the words, she added, "Get out. I've had it with men and their dumbass ways."

Stunned, astonished, he roared, "Then want *do* you want?" Frustration apparent in his loud voice, he stared her down.

Faith caught the next sob before it burst out. "If you have to ask, it won't matter. Leave."

"Honey..."

"No. Don't you honey me! Not when your narrow-mindedness infuriates me." Anger flooded. She relished the emotion. "Don't look at me like that either. You're a stupid, stupid man, and I want you to leave."

Steven's beseeching stare turned hard, and he did exactly as she'd requested. Biting back an oath, he stomped to the hallway and slammed the door behind him.

Faith bit her lip, wanting to stop the sobs choking her, but it would be like trying to dam the ocean. Once her crying stopped, she massaged her chest, easing the pain a little, and she made plans.

I don't need any man in my life. From now on, when he visits with Raoul, I'll go into the other room or − or I'll go for a walk. It's more than time they fended for themselves an hour a day.

Making up her mind and feeling better for it, she unpacked the groceries they'd dumped in the kitchen earlier. Then she checked Raoul, who slept soundly, and sat near him in the chair.

Was she kidding herself? Could she survive, seeing Steven every day, knowing his opinion of her? Was it time she found a new life?

The sweetness building between them had blinded her to the fact that he had no respect for her. How could she form a relationship based only on sexual gratification?

She had no doubt he wanted her as much as she yearned to again feel his lips kissing hers and his hands on her body. After all her years in the business, she could tell when a man found her physically and sexually attractive. But then most men in her past didn't try and conceal their lust, just the opposite.

Oh, who was she trying to kid? She'd fallen for the guy. Everything about him delighted her. As a person used to responsibilities, a man in charge, respected by most people he met, she looked up to him. That had never happened between her and Raoul.

Next to the charismatic businessman, Steven Corella, her Raoul was like an overgrown loveable boy. She'd totally adored him for his sweet ways and accepting heart. But it wasn't meant to be. She'd lost him during the worst days of her life, and she'd come to accept it wasn't meant to be.

Now she had another Raoul to love, a tiny baby who needed her and who she needed even more. Could she leave him to get away from Steven?

Not yet, while he was so dependent on her. But, if things didn't change, she'd have to rethink that choice. Before she could give in to the building wall of despair, the doorbell rang and her heart slammed into her throat while panic broke out over her body.

Not the next-door drunken dope again. *Please, not now.* The doorbell rang again.

Surging to her feet, her rage red hot, she stomped to the door to get rid of the cheating prick once and for all.

I'll give him a piece of my mind he won't soon forget, stupid ass.

Angry, peephole forgotten, she whipped open the door and began her rant.

"If you don't leave me alone I'll call the police and press..." A male image materialized through the mist of red-hot fury, and she let out a squeaky sob. Then she threw herself into his arms.

"Sam!"

Chapter Nine

Sam patted her back and squeezed her to him. "Hey, Sunshine. I'm glad you're happy to see me, but I believe we need to have us a little powwow."

Relief left her weakened. The weeping started again, though she tried her best to shut it down.

Lifting her into his arms, he carried her over to the sofa and sat her down, and then made room for himself. "Okay, little one, time to tell Uncle Sam what's going on so he can help you."

Faith reached for his hand and clung. This man with the dangerous eyes and kind heart had befriended her as well as their friend, Cassi Santino. Working undercover as a bartender at the Lipstick Club where she'd kept men happy upstairs, Sam knew exactly what she'd done for a living. Her notorious background had been obvious. And still, he'd only treated her with respect and a gentleness she'd welcomed.

Unlike most other males in her past, he'd never made any unwanted moves or tried taking advantage of her because of her occupation. Over the last few months, as they'd waited for Cassi and Trace's wedding, she'd discovered his soft core and had come to love him dearly.

"Don't be angry, okay?" She knew he had a temper when riled.

"Now why would I be angry?"

"Because your eyes are spitting bullets and your jaw is hard. I know that look. I've seen you like this before."

"What look?" He grinned, working her, calming her, trying to pull the wool over her eyes.

"Stop, Sam. You really don't have to be upset. I'm going to handle the situation on my own. It's time I toughened up. You and I both know if I hadn't been such a weakling when I worked at the club, Raoul might be alive today."

During the interrogation she'd had with the FBI agents, because of Raoul's death and Leni's involvement, Faith had told Sam everything. About how she'd called on her friend to take on a responsibility she'd been too weak to handle. She'd sent Leni to warn Raoul that the *Armas* gang were going to hurt him rather than go herself.

At the time, she'd been convinced that no one would have listened to her, and she'd never have been able to stop them from punishing him. In her mind, Leni was stronger and smarter and would step up. Except, as it turned out, Leni had been forced to pull the trigger and Raoul had died.

"Sam, I have to stop letting other people do my dirty work. After Raoul died, Cassi changed. She grew up, became strong and went after the killers. So if she can do that, why can't I?"

Sam took her face in his large hands and made her look into his searching eyes.

"Sugar, I have no doubt you can do what you make up your mind to do. But understand this, not everyone has the same incentives to change like Cass, or the ability and background to make things work. She's a fighter, born with the skill. You aren't."

Faith thought about his words. Her eyes roamed the lean face that many women would find attractive. His longish silver tail had disappeared and the shorter, now wavy haircut gave him a cowboy kind of look. All he needed was the hat and one could be forgiven their conclusion. It made her wonder if he might be working undercover on a ranch, not that she'd ask.

"Sam, if you knew that a woman was getting harassed by a neighbor, what would you suggest she do?"

As he surveyed her face, Sam's head tilted sideways. "I'd say to forcefully shove your knee where his brain hung."

Giggling, a sudden levity that surprised her, she grimaced and admitted. "I actually did that already."

"And he's still trying to mess with you?"

"Earlier, he pounded on my door, and Steven scared him away. But he said he'd be back later." She shuddered. "I'm expecting him anytime. Yesterday, I went to borrow a vase for the bouquet I caught from Cassie. There's a girl called Maria who lives across the hall. We've talked a few times, and she's nice. I've given her coffee when she ran out, and I knew she wouldn't mind me borrowing from her."

"And..."

"Unknown to me, she's visiting her mom. Her fiancé answered the door and recognized me as one of his favorites from the club. After Raoul died, I gave up caring about what happened to me, Sam. A few of the men sensed it and took advantage, got mean and pushed the limits."

Sam's droll reply made her smile. "Some men are a fucking waste of skin."

"Ain't that the truth?" She grinned and continued. "I told him I'd moved on but in his drunken dopiness, he'd only heard I'd moved here and it was business as usual. He made a move, tried to force me and I had no choice."

"Good girl. You did right. If he tries anything again, you let me know. Scum like him need to understand, it's against the law to force their unsolicited attentions on an unwilling lady."

"That's just it, Sam. I don't want to call for help.

I want to make him mind his manners myself."

Sam held both her hands to make her listen. "Baby, I know what you're thinking, but you have to understand. No two people are alike. Cass is Cass and you are Sunshine. See? Even the names are reflective of the person. There are people who care about you and are more than willing and better equipped, to fight the battles you can't. Do you understand?"

Deflated, Faith nodded. "I suppose you're right. I have to accept my limitations—"

Pounding on the door stopped her mid-sentence.

"It's him." Blood drained from her face and the wild burst of adrenalin stimulated a flight response. Her resolve started to shrivel up until she recognized her weakness.

Sam stood, his movements measured yet full of resolve.

Her hand held his arm. "Let me at least try to handle it, okay?"

"Sure, Sunshine. But I'll be listening from right behind the door."

She nodded – her relief obvious and her gratitude showing. "Okay."

Once Sam was in place and nodded, she opened the door to find the drunken pest waving her monitor around like it was the extension of his finger.

"Look here, Sunshine. My money is as good as

anyone's. I just need a little company. I even brought back your property." Slurring his words and talking smack, he appeared rumpled and messy and stinkin' drunk.

"Thank you." Ignoring the rest of his speech, Faith acknowledged the last sentence and reached to take the article.

Yanking it out of her reach, pretending a playfulness that failed, he sputtered, "Not so quick, babe. Let me come in and keep you company. Then you can have this back."

Stamping her foot, Faith leaned forward. "You're not coming in here, so get that through your stupid head. And if you don't give me my property, I'll call the police and have you charged with harassment. You want Maria to find out what you're up to when she's away? Because I'm just the girl to tell her, you hear?" Her voice louder than she'd intended, Faith felt pride in her forcefulness. Sam would hear her sticking up for herself and that mattered.

"You bitch." Transforming from the playful drunk to his true character, he acted. Before she knew what happened, the souse pushed closer and forced her backwards. One hand grabbed her slender neck while the other lifted to punch, only his fist never made the connection.

Instead, Sam connected with him, more than once. And before the creep could gather enough wits to protect himself; Sam pulled out his I.D.

and spit out, "F.B.I. You're under arrest for assault, breaking and entering, and for being the kind of mean-assed son of a bitch I'd just as soon shoot. So don't tempt me."

Shaken yet relieved, a variety of emotions exploded inside Faith. Fear fought with self-disgust. Her weak inability to defend herself had become obvious now. Then relief seeped into the mix for not having to take another beating.

God, Faith, why couldn't you be strong for once in your pathetic life?

Yet when Sam asked her if she'd press charges, hesitation crept in.

A steely stare from Sam had the tilt-a-whirl of her mind slowing until a final decision brought it to a dead stop. "Yes. I'll press charges. He can't get away with behaving like an animal."

Sam's lavish grin wasn't often seen. It warmed her all the way through. "Good girl. I'm proud of you."

When the other man tried to rise, Sam kicked him back down to the floor. "You! Stay down! Don't piss me off any more than you already have." He hugged Faith and whispered. "You tried, sugar. But some men are just such animals."

He hauled the now whining animal with the bloody mouth to his feet and pushed him into the outer hallway in front of him.

She heard Sam's message prior to closing and locking the door.

"I'll be in touch."

Chapter Ten

Before Faith had enough time to wallow in self-disgust, Raoul woke up and demanded her attendance.

"Hi, dumpling." She lifted him in her arms and buried her face in his sweet-smelling baby's neck. Nuzzling, she spoke low. "Your pathetic nanny failed once again, tiger. Strong and self-sufficient – pooh. I'm nothing but a big wuss!"

She held the baby away so she could look into his face. His slobbering grin had her smiling. "I don't know what you see in me Raoul, my little man. I truly don't."

A recital of baby sounds greeted her words while tiny arms waved around as if he had an opponent close to punch. His antics made her laugh. Heart filled to overflowing, tremendous joy burst forth. Gathering him in close, she whispered, "How could I ever leave you?"

***

Steven fumed.

There was no other word to use. On the way to his office, he revisited their final scene and felt both confused and pissed over the way Faith had behaved. For the gazillionth time, he re-examined her hurtful words. They'd been in reaction to something he'd said.

He'd lit the fuse. He knew it. And yet he didn't understand why. What more did she want from him? He'd told her that he'd forgiven her past. And if she'd have let him speak further, he would have explained that they never had to speak of it again. They would start anew and see what happened.

Yet, if he was honest, forgiving was one thing, but could he ever forget? It was a lot to ask of a guy – to stop his mind from visualizing his beautiful blonde nanny being paid to satisfy other men – hordes of other men... using, and most likely, abusing her body. Over and over again.

God! The incoming, unstoppable images made him want to hurl. He wiped his face and grabbed the nearby bottle of water. Mouth dry, stomach soured, his mind searched for help. He needed to talk to someone he trusted. Dealing with the problem alone, he'd scored dismally.

His mind shifted from person to person until it alighted on the men in law enforcement who he respected – Sam, Trace and Michael. They'd have a lot more knowledge of the dark side and the characters who live there. Could they help him get his head on straight?

Picking up his phone, he placed a call and found he was in luck. "Hi Trace, Steven Corella here. I guess I'm in luck. You and Cassi haven't left on your honeymoon yet."

"Hi, Steve. Plans are in the works for next week. I was forced to take on my new position as Chief earlier than anticipated and it's messed with the schedule, but Cassi is being a sweetheart and not riding me too hard."

"I heard on the news about Hank Lester's heart attack. How's he feeling now?"

"It's amazing what a five-way bypass can do for a man who can't breathe. He's gonna pull through. So, what's up?"

"I have a small personal problem, with Faith actually, and some good male common sense from people who know her better might help me see things more clearly. Any chance you and Michael can join me for a drink later at the Center bar here in the Casino – maybe after work?"

"Sure, I'm good. I'll get a hold of Michael and see what he's up to."

"Just have them page me when you show up."

"Fine, I'm thinking it'll be around six or so."

"Perfect. Thanks, man. I'm in trouble here, and no matter which way I turn, it's only me blathering on with myself and making little sense."

"No problem, bro. See you later."

Experiencing warmth from being treated like he mattered, Steven pulled out a card from his wallet.

Now all he needed to do was call Sam.

"Hey, Steve. Good to hear from you. In fact, you're just the guy I wanted to touch base with."

"That's why I'm calling. Do you have time to grab a beer tonight around six?"

"Shit! I'd make time, but I'm on a job. I'll try and catch up with you tomorrow."

"Okay. That's fine."

"If it's important I can probably make some arrangements."

"No. I wanted to talk about Faith, that's all."

"No shit! That's what I wanted to cover with you too."

"Sounds ominous. Something I should know?"

"It depends on you, but I'd say so. In case you haven't figured it out yet man, that chick's one sweet lady."

"I know." And he did know... okay, maybe he didn't. But another validation about Faith's goodness, and from a man he respected, made him feel even more like a shit for dithering.

"See you tomorrow."

Steven had a bad feeling that Sam's news wouldn't be good. In fact, he almost called him back, but his assistant's buzzing intervened.

"Natalie Cross is here and insists on coming in. She says she's Raoul's mother."

Shit! What could she want? His first impulse was to send her away but curiosity got the better of him. "Send her in, but if she hasn't left in ten minutes, call me."

"Okay. Between you and me, she doesn't look very good. Just sayin'... I'd be careful if I were you, boss."

Having total trust in John's opinion, his assistant was discreet but discerning; he thanked him and wondered at the shivers of apprehension that played havoc with his sudden nervousness.

Considering at one time he thought he loved Raoul's mother enough to marry her, it shocked him at how different he felt about her now. His ardour had died a quick and painless death after she'd been willing to give up her baby for twenty thousand dollars.

Shaking his head, disgust began forming like it always did whenever he thought about her selfishness. Only a greedy, hard-hearted bitch would do something so vile. Him and Raoul were well rid of her.

Interrupting his thoughts, the door opened and John ushered in a person he'd never have recognized if he'd passed her on the street. His former girlfriend had been lovely in her over-the-top, model-stylish way.

She'd had aspirations for the stage and had always looked ready for a photo shoot – until she got pregnant. Gaining an enormous amount of unnecessary weight, depression over the changes in her body messed with her head.

Yet even the bitchy, blotchy-faced, overweight

pregnant girl with scraped-back hair and wearing a constant frown couldn't compare to the person weaving in front of him now.

"Steven. I-I need to see you. I think I'm sick."

"You're high. Trust me, there's a difference."

Seemingly confused, Natalie collapsed into the chair placed in front of his desk. She withdrew a disgusting looking overly used tissue from the pocket of her ripped, grubby jeans and blew her nose, missing a line of snot that stuck to her chin. Thankfully, the second swipe cleared it away.

Older, discolored bruises appeared on her neck, hands and high on her right cheek. Faded slightly, one turned her eye bloodshot and a nearby scab appeared infected.

He remembered how she'd driven him crazy; waiting for her while she'd fiddled with her long, glowing auburn mane. A perfectionist, every hair had to be in place in the elaborate styles she'd fixed. Today, the greasy mess was gathered where half had been pulled into a tail and the rest straggled every which way around her face.

Sickened and saddened by her appearance, he asked, "What do you want, Natalie?"

Trying to focus, she mumbled, "I'm with another guy, now. He's different than you, Steve. He says I shouldn't have signed away my rights to the baby, and... and I need to come back and re-renegotiate. 'Cause I love my baby."

"You don't love anyone but yourself, Natalie,

certainly not our son." Controlling his anger was much easier than overcoming his disgust. "You couldn't wait to get your hands on that twenty-thousand dollar check from the lawyer for carrying Raoul. You certainly aren't getting a penny more. So go tell your new boyfriend to back off."

"He says I can get a lawyer. He knows someone who'll fight for me to get visiting rights. The courts are always on the birth mother's side. That's what he says."

"Not so, Natalie, especially when the mother's obviously a heavy drug user."

Shrugging off his truth, she continued to push. "Steven you don't know him."

Worry formed and began creeping in. It made his voice harder than he'd meant it to be. His usual skills to talk down a client had fled, which left him raging with fatherly protectiveness. Naked without his business-like armor, he clenched his fists and forced the calm.

"What is it you really want, Natalie?"

"I want to see him."

"Him – who?"

"The baby."

"Hell, you never even stuck around in the hospital long enough to learn his name. It's Raoul."

"Good. Fine. It's nice. So, what do you say?"

"No."

"But... I've got rights."

"You signed them away. I have the sealed court

documents. They give me full custody." Suddenly the pealing of his phone made him jump and broke into the building tension.

"Not now, John. Hold my calls." While he talked, he watched her scrutinize her fingernails without actually focusing on anything. *Shit!* It gave him the creeps.

As soon as he hung up, she started in again. "What if you just help me? Like, give me money – a loan? Maybe I could talk him into leaving town. We'd be out of your way for good."

"A loan."

"Yeah. Like maybe ten thousand. Then I know I could get him to drop the whole idea."

"No."

"No?" That caught her attention. "You want we should fight in court?"

"There'll be no fight, no court... nothing, Natalie. To manage that, you need money to pay for a lawyer, and I'd be willing to bet that you haven't a cent left of the payment I gave you after Raoul was born."

A crafty look appeared on the mottled yet pale face in front of him. She seemed to re-enter the real world long enough to throw down the gauntlet.

"He has an idea how to get the money, you know. Don't underestimate him, you won't like the consequences."

"From the marks on your face, you've dealt with

them first hand, and I'm sorry about that. I hate to think of you in the clutches of evident scum like him. But you're a grown woman, capable of making choices. So, I think you'd better leave, Natalie, and take this message to the schmuck. I won't pay you one fucking red cent."

As if John held a glass up to the door, listening in on their conversation, it opened and his assistant waited to escort Natalie from the office.

Looking completely dumbstruck, Natalie cowered in her chair, regressing back to the weakling who'd first appeared. "No. You have to give me money. I need you to. I-I can't leave without it. He'll be unhappy with me."

"Honey, that's not my problem. John will show you out."

Before she knew what had happened, John manually lifted her from her chair and frog-marched her out the door. All Steven heard were her arguments echoing. "You don't understand. I need the money. You have to help me."

Frazzled big time, the fearful voice receding still prickling his nerves, he reached for the phone.

"Hello."

"Faith? How's everything at the apartment?"

Puzzlement rang in her soft voice. "Steven? Are you okay? What's wrong?"

Overcome with relief, and feeling slightly foolish about his anxiety, he toned down his voice. "It's nothing, Faith. I just had a visit from Raoul's mother, Natalie. She's hooked on some crazy drugs and they're making her weird. It got me rattled."

"No doubt. What did she want?"

"Money. What else? If she comes there, don't answer the door."

"Okay. I won't."

"Wait, do you know what she looks like?"

"Just from the pictures she left of you two together."

"A thousand years ago. She's nothing like the girl in those photos so be careful. If she bothers you, call me right away."

"I will. Thanks for warning me."

"I'll be by to see Raoul a little later than my usual time. But I'll be there."

Her voice lost the pleasant tone and left him frowning.

"Okay."

Click.

He noticed she didn't end the call in her usual sweet way by saying, "We'll be waiting."

He felt sad.

Chapter Eleven

It took Faith hours to shake off the trepidation that started as soon as she'd heard the tone of Steven's voice. Just the thought of a female who could possibly give up the rights to such a beautiful child, blew her mind. The idea of her coming to their apartment ramped up her protective instincts.

That bitch wasn't getting near Raoul.

Slumped in a fancy baby rocker that Leni had bought for him, Raoul swung his arms happily. Occasionally, he bumped the hanging mobiles and cooed at the colorful animal he liked the best. Happy as long as Faith stayed close, he showed off his new-found ability to make the bunny spin, and then went back to his favorite pastime of finding his mouth with his searching fingers.

Laughing, she bent to kiss the dark fuzz on his head and cleaned away the baby gear spread around the room. She liked to have everything tidy before Steven showed up... including her.

Tonight, she'd berated herself the whole time she spent in the bathroom, applying makeup and fixing her hair. *Why're you bothering? The man looks at you and sees a whore. Give it up!*

Only she couldn't.

Lying, telling herself it was a matter of pride, she worked away and after an hour, her beautiful hair shone, gleaming golden highlights that blazed from the decorative crystals of the light fixture hanging over the mirror.

Covering over the shadows in her eyes with makeup applied perfectly, she added the pink lipstick she knew suited her best and then dressed in her favorite blue sundress.

Raoul sat in his chair, watching the whole procedure. "What do you think, little man? Can I even compete with all the sexy women he's surrounded by every day?"

The baby's head tilted to the side and she could have sworn he winked, even if she knew better.

Laughing, she added. "You're very good for my self-confidence, you know that handsome?"

The doorbell rang and she grasped the handle of the chair and picked Raoul up, carrying him with her to the hallway. Placing him against the wall so he wouldn't be in sight of her visitor, she took the caution of glancing through the peephole.

Within minutes, she'd thrown open the door and reached for the waiting arms. "Cassi." Delight rang in her voice. "I'm so glad to see you. Come in."

"Hey, lady. Trace left a message to say him and Michael were having a drink with Steven at the bar before he came home. I figured what's good for the guys, is good for the gals. Right? So, us gals are having our own cocktail hour here with you. Leni's coming in a little while."

Thrilled to have her friends close today, she moved in to hug Cassi one more time. Only she clung.

Cassi, more than willing to accommodate, patted her back and then gently pulled back. "Spit it out, brat. What's up?"

Totally trusting the dark-haired girl with the gorgeous, slanted eyes that could turn from the softest baby blue to glacier chips in seconds, Faith accepted the bottle of white wine and closed the door behind Cassi.

Cassi stepped in, and a noise had her turning in Raoul's direction. "Hello my favorite little man." Still slender and agile from her work-outs at the gym and in the boxing ring, Cassi reached for Raoul who began flirting the minute he heard her voice. Lifting him in her arms, she followed Faith into the living room. All the way, she nuzzled and kissed soft baby cheeks.

Faith, recognizing Cassi's work-out top peeking through the light jacket, turned on her friend. "You're dressed for the gym. Please tell me you're not still acting as Leni's sparring partner? Trace must be livid.'

"For heaven's sake, not you too. I'm pregnant, not terminal. The baby is still a tiny little button deep inside and totally protected. I'd have no problem being in the ring, but you'd think between Rusty and Trace, I should be in a wheel chair. Bah! Men."

Faith burst out laughing. "You're spoiled and you love it, so don't try fooling a fool, baby. I agree with them. There're a lot of people who can work with Leni now. She's much less aggressive than she used to be, right?"

"Oh, baby. You got that wrong!" Cassi shook her head, her short black curls grown to all one length, bounced around her beautiful face. "My sweet sister's a dynamo in the ring, you know that. She scares off most of her willing sparring partners. But Rusty keeps a tight rein on her, and she behaves... mostly." The affectionate tone in Cassi's voice told its own story. She obviously adored her sister.

"You miss it. I can see it in your eyes."

"Yeah, I guess I do. It kept me focused and clear-headed while using my strength. My body misses it the most. I do some shadow-boxing in the basement gym, but it isn't the same."

"Now with the baby on the way, have you decided whether you're going to stay with your classes to get your law degree?"

"As long as I can. I found out the university has day care options, and if I keep my hours flexible, it'll work."

"Hold It! What day care? No way, Cass. The only day care you need for that precious bundle is Faith's day care. Raoul and I will be happy to look after his little cousin, won't we buddy?" Faith leaned forward to tickle Raoul's chin, and his sudden beaming, toothless grin and cooing agreement made her laugh. "See. He's all for it."

Cassi's sigh of relief was loud, which told Faith that it was something she'd been fretting over.

"God, Faith. Seriously? You'll look after the baby? I wanted to ask you so badly, Trace too, but it seemed to be expecting too much from you, having two little ones to babysit. And what if Steven doesn't like the idea? "

The determined expression mirrored what Faith felt inside. "Truly, it's just the opposite. I'd love to have the baby. And you leave that Steven to me."

Cassi picked up on something in her tone. Faith saw her eyes narrow, and she drilled her with a 'what's-up' stare. "Spill, sunshine. Something's going on."

"If you get the glasses and open the wine, I'll change our bambino and feed him his bottle while we talk."

Cassi backed off and added, "Fine. But how about we switch jobs? I'm gonna need the practice."

Within a short time, the girls were back in the living room, Faith curled in the corner of the sofa with her legs under her and a glass of wine in her hand, while Cassi cuddled Raoul as she fed him from the bottle.

Cassi started the conversation. "Now, tell me what's put those shadows in your eyes? I can feel waves of sadness all the way over here."

Faith, barely in control, knew tears were trying to force their way out. She fought hard and pushed them back. "Please don't get the wrong idea, Cass. I'm upset, and a little scared, but it's not self-pity. I just don't know what to do."

"Do about what?"

"I had a fight with Steven earlier. I told him to leave. It just dawned on me now, I kicked him out of his own place." Faith looked distressed when the thought hit home.

"Hold it! It's not his home. It's his apartment. This is your home, yours and Raoul's. Plus, I'm pretty sure if you... ahh kicked him out; you had one helluva good reason."

Faith's face broke into a smile. "My loyal fan. Thank you. I thought I had a good reason at the time. But now I'm not so sure. He told me he'd forgiven my past, and all I could think of were the words you and Leni drilled into my head at the wedding. I don't need his forgiveness, right?"

"Fucking right! You've never harmed a living soul, Faith. You have to start understanding the reasons why you went in the direction you did. After that, when you see clearly what led you to doing what you did, you have to accept that it was a part of your past. It's over. You're a different person now."

"Now, I'm a good person."

"Hell girl, you've always been a *good* person, that's what got you into this mess in the first place. From what you've told me and Leni, it's that big heart of yours – protecting your mother – that started you on this path. Now she's gone, all future choices are yours." Cassi purposely forced them both to look at the baby by holding aloft the sleeping child. "You chose life. And to nurture another in need. Only this time, it's my nephew. Can you imagine how happy that makes me? Every time I think of Precious here with you, I pretty much groan with relief."

Laughing now, feeling better, Faith admitted, "I can't seem to stop putting myself down. I know it's dumb, you and Leni have worked on me enough. It's clear and wrong. But when I examine myself through other's criticizing judgements, I see what they imagine, a bad seed, a whore... a-a misfit."

"You didn't today."

"No. I guess I didn't. The words he used, *he'd forgiven me*, struck a chord, and I remembered Leni giving me shit for saying the exact same thing the other day. I told him I didn't need his forgiveness and to leave."

Laying the baby on his fluffy quilt between them on the couch, Cassi squatted down next to Faith and took her face between her hands. "You did right, Faith. Never, ever let anyone put you into that slot again. And by that, I'm including you. You aren't what you do; it's just a job, a way to survive. If I'm wrong, then I'm the meanest bitch alive according to some of the news articles after the fight with Ariana."

"You are not." Without hesitation, Faith burst out in support. "That's just stupid."

"See? I'm not what I do. Neither were you." A doorbell pealing had both girls twisting toward the sound. "I'll let Leni in, you mop up or she'll know something's up, and we won't be able to stop her from wanting to kick the shit out of that misguided man of yours."

Laughing and swiping at her damp cheeks, Faith said, "You're right. Thanks Cass. You always know what I need to hear."

"Just make him understand the "whys" for what you did, and if that bastard still sits in judgement, you call me, and I'll *help* Leni kick the shit outta him."

Faith laughed – contentment renewed. While waiting, she wiped her face, blew her nose and loosened her shoulders, blessing the day she met Cassi. Though their first meeting had ended in a bitch fight with other upstairs girls, and her losing Raoul's baby, it also led to her finding this new beginning.

One worth fighting for...

Chapter
Twelve

Cassi, expecting Leni, never thought to check the peephole. It was a huge mistake. Once she'd opened the door it was too late. The guy, holding the pizza, tossed the box aside and the cloth he'd hidden flashed toward her face.

Instincts from her years of training kicked in. Grabbing the arm, she propelled it forward and twisted it away from her.

Built like a toolshed, the man overpowered her easily and pushed her through the hallway into the room where Faith sat frozen.

"Get Raoul into the bedroom." Cass barked the command as she fought the beating. Her fists, plowing into the guy's stomach had no impact, and neither did her kick to his groin.

Falling back on her martial art's stuff, she aimed her leg high, did a twirl and when he arced backward in retreat, she pulled one of her fancy moves and slid to the floor inches from the backhand he'd aimed at her face.

When she drove her fist upwards to plow into his most vulnerable area, he sensed her intention and made a countermove that pinned her head between his legs.

While she struggled to get loose, she saw Faith in full battle with a dark-haired female who was trying to pull Raoul out of her arms. Cussing and swearing, not worrying about the frail child, the crazy bitch clawed and hit like a woman possessed.

In full protective mode, Faith took punch after punch but held onto the baby clutched against her chest. She never fought back; instead she took every punishing blow as she protected her precious bundle and staggered toward the safety of the bathroom and a door with a lock.

Cassi's strength waned from lack of oxygen, and she used the last of it to bite the leg she could reach. Male screams joining those of a furious baby added to the unreality of the moment.

With only few precious seconds of freedom, she dove back into the battle with renewed energy. Her opponent trampled her, uncaring, needing to shake her free. Before she could roll to safety, the ungodly pain from fifty thousand volts in her back drove her to her knees. Convulsing, frozen in place, stunned and unable to move, she collapsed.

"Nat, here, use this on the bitch." The male, standing above her, yelled to the woman. Then he threw her the Taser.

Now in a fog of agony, Cassi heard Faith's excruciating screams. Even louder, she heard, "Let go, bitch. Jesus, Hal, she's not letting go."

"For fuck's sake," Hal stepped over Cassi and drove his fist into Faith's cheek. Struggling, yet having no muscle control, Cassi tried grabbing his leg but her hands were useless. The kick aimed to her head stopped her dead.

Receding howls from an alarmed Raoul rang in her ears before all went quiet.

Chapter Thirteen

A favorite with the customers, the Center bar with its round tables, orange plush chairs and brown leather couches pulsed with casino sounds and slot-machine noises in the background. Beside the array of monitors offering games and gambling, the bartenders were kept busy as well as the servers.

Being a boss and well-known, Steven warranted special treatment and got it from the pretty waitress who smilingly pointed out the reserved sign in a quiet corner. "Saved your favorite table, Boss. Thanks for warning us you'd be stopping by."

"No problem, Nicole. Just bring me a Corona, whatever Trace wants and some of those salty nuts." Trace nodded his agreement with the beer choice and followed Steven who stopped and turned back.

"There'll be another friend joining us, so if a big, good-looking bald cop shows up, send him over."

Grinning, Nicole teased. "If he's good-looking, can't I just keep him for myself?"

Chuckling, Steven answered. "Sorry, he's already taken."

Flipping her hair over her shoulders, the red-headed beauty grimaced playfully, "Just my luck." She bounced away, taking her teasing good spirits with her.

Steven, knowing they'd be interrupted as soon as she returned with the tray of drinks, opened with a safe subject. "How's Cassi feeling? I remember Natalie, that's Raoul's mother, in her first trimester." He shivered on purpose. "That girl wasn't the cheerful type at the best of times, but I got to thinking she'd been possessed by a zombie alien with a really bad temper. I never knew there were that many swear words to describe a man."

Laughing, Trace still managed to look smug. "Cassi's – Cassi. Nothing fazes that girl. She's in such good shape from all her training that she's sailing through like a trooper. What bugs her is my overprotective anxieties. Every time I make a completely legitimate, polite suggestion, it drives her bananas."

Knowing exactly what Trace was getting at, yet interested to hear his response, Steven questioned. "Like?"

"Like sit on the couch and watch TV all day long. And sweetheart, eat as many chocolates as you want."

Cracking up, Steven shook his head. "I'm amazed you're still walking, man. You *must* be driving her batty."

Trace picked up the beer Nicole had just delivered and grinned. "She gets pretty chippy, but curtailing her activities is my job as an expecting daddy, right?"

"If you say so! I'm not the person you want to ask about women. I've never had any luck in that arena."

Trace's cell rang to interrupt the conversation. He swiped it to open the call. "Chief Sloan here." He listened and nodded, his eyes narrowed with concentration. "Yeah, okay Mike. Sorry to miss you. Keep me updated."

Steven watched the big man in front of him as he handled his call and picked up instantly that likely Michael had called to cancel.

"Sorry, Steve, Mike's not gonna be able to make it. He just caught a case."

"Sorry to hear that. It means someone's in trouble."

"Yeah, we're kinda short at the department because of the shooting that happened yesterday. I spent most of the day at the site and the carnage made me wonder at the world today. High-caliber rifles killing people and crazies who own them always get the same reaction from me and the other police members. We can only act within the law, so until someone above my pay grade smartens up and makes necessary changes, we do what we can."

"I'd never have your job. Being in that much danger, day after day, must wear on a man."

"Nah! It's all part of the... Shit, who'm I trying to kid. It's tough. And as the years go by, it gets tougher. The men who work for the department fight every day to keep it together. Now that I'm in the hot seat, I've come to realize that the complaints I had about Hank Lester when he did the job, were bogus and bullshit. The man's hands were tied in the same way I'm finding that mine are. Between the Mayor and City Council, the media and the various associations that want a voice in how things are run... and the union, it's a daily, badly organized shit-show."

"Will you be able to get away for your honeymoon; I know you had to put it off once. Cassi must be pretty understanding if she's still letting you in at night."

"She is. I'm a lucky bastard, and I know it. But then so are you, dude. That Faith is one sweet lady."

***

Steven felt stunned. The sentence reverberated in his head. Trace saw Faith as a lady – pure and simple, same as Sam. He didn't sense any prejudice for her previous lifestyle from the cop in front of him. No lack of respect. Just affection and liking.

He had to know for certain. He needed to understand. Diving right in, he asked, "Man, you speak of Faith with such esteem, and yet you know what she did not that long ago."

"So, that's what this pow-wow is all about."

"I'm a mess. Look, I'm crazy about the girl, but I went to the Lipstick Club and even visited the upstairs salon for as long as I could stomach it. Picturing Faith there, with those sad individuals made me want to puke. I drove around for hours trying to get my head straight. And I did. Or at least, I thought so." Steven drank a goodly amount from his bottle, giving Trace a chance to kick in but the man remained silent.

"So..."

"So... I took Faith shopping today at the mall and I swear to you, Trace, I never intended it to happen. Yet every man who looked at her, I suspected might be a previous client. And man, did she get a lot of looks."

"She's a beautiful girl. It happens."

"Right, I know. I worked hard to overcome that shit, and when we got home, I told her that I forgave her. That's when she kicked me out." Defeated, not able to stop his self-pity, he searched Trace's expression to see what he was thinking.

Interest showed and nothing else. Cops wore masks that covered their thoughts. Ingrained from training and years on the job, Trace's face gave him no clue to his thoughts.

On the other hand, his words spoke volumes. "You told her you forgive her?"

"Yes. I'm nuts about her, and I want us to have a future. With her past between us, I felt it needed to be said."

"Man, you are one of the dumbest fuckers I've met in a long time and trust me; I've run up against some dillies."

The words cut him in half. Envisioning rivers of blood draining from his emasculated body, Steven dropped his head. *Shit!* Based on Trace's sudden expressive disgust, he'd screwed up big-time.

Chapter Fourteen

Coming to, Cassi heard heartbroken sobs first. Then she heard Leni's howl of outrage.

"What the fuck?"

The horror in Leni's voice sucked her out of the safe cocoon of darkness she'd experienced. Her head felt like a boot was still embedded, which prompted her to investigate.

That's when she saw the blood. As soon as her brain registered what it was, the pungent, metallicky smell from the fresh wound cleared her brain.

I'm bleeding. He kicked me. The sick bastard kicked me.

***

Faith tried to crawl closer to Cassi, but ungodly pain rampaging in different directions throughout her body made it impossible. Floating between consciousness and a dream state, she understood a nightmare had occurred, she just couldn't clearly remember. One thing that was clear, her body hurt everywhere, especially her face.

Suddenly, Leni appeared. She crouched beside Faith, and the rage plastered on her face helped clear away some of the fog from Faith's scattered brain. It was also the brutal moment when reality hit.

My God, Raoul! Oh, God... NO!

Those monsters had abducted her beautiful charge, the baby who'd saved her life when he'd hauled her back from the murky abyss of despair. She loved Raoul, cherished him as much as if she'd given birth to him.

Unable to stop her mind from going back to the earlier scene, it washed over her in waves of horror.

They'd kidnapped him. She'd tried, but hadn't been able to stop them. They just carried him off.

Screaming...

A wail began deep in her stomach and by the time it broke through her lips, it rang with indescribable panic, bordering on insanity.

"Jesus, Faith. You're freakin' me out. Calm down. It's Leni. I'm here with you. I've called the paramedics and Michael. Can you tell me where it hurts?"

"Everywhere. They took Raoul."

"They? They who? Who took Raoul? Don't cry so hard, Faith, I can't understand what you're saying."

***

Leni had arrived to an open door, a smell of pepperoni pizza oozing from the box on the floor and a sense of doom. Instincts to be careful made her step slowly. Dread, heavy on her shoulders, she called out, "Cass? Faith?"

Sounds, like an animal in pain, drew her to the living room. That's when she saw the carnage. Shock struck first. Normal breathing impossible, she choked as she surveyed the damage.

Cassi lay face down on the floor, blood soaking her hair and pooling around her on the floor. Nearby, Faith hugged herself in a fetal position; bruises appeared red and raw on her face and arms.

Leni ran to Cassi, who was closest, and did what she'd seen others do on TV. Careful not to step on any evidence, she felt for her neck pulse and breathed a deep sigh when it registered strong.

She withdrew her cellphone from her pocket. It slid to the floor from her shaking hands. Words she muttered didn't really register. "*Come on. Oh, God. Shit!*"

She scooped it up and pressed a number she knew would take her directly to the man she needed more now than she'd ever needed anyone before. Faith moved and drew her attention.

Hitting the speaker, she let the phone slide to the floor so she could help Faith.

Coiled, her arms hugging her chest, Faith looked like an overgrown baby in the womb. Or someone whose heart had been ripped to shreds and the subsequent wound was more than she could bear.

Tears clouded Leni's vision. Her stomach clenched to keep down the hamburger she'd ordered and scarfed on the way over. Hands shaking, she bent to touch, soothe....

"Faith, honey, let me help you. Can you move? No, don't get all the way up. Just lie there until Michael gets here. He's on his way."

As if her prayer had been answered, a male voice sounded loudly over her phone's speaker.

"Hey, baby. What's up?"

Sanity!

"Michael. Oh, My God! It's Faith and Cassi. I just got to Faith's. They've been attacked. There's blood everywhere."

"What the hell happened?" Stunned, upset, angry were words too ordinary to describe the vehemence she heard in his voice.

"I don't know. Hold on, Cassi's moving. She's alive and so is Faith. Can you send an ambulance?"

"I'm only a few blocks away, Leni. I'm calling the paramedics right now." Leni heard the sirens start up and his voice giving orders. "Do what you can for them but don't move anything. Try and get the girls to stay where they are in case they have internal injuries. I'm pulling up now. Hang on; I'll be up there with you in a few minutes."

Faith, seeming to have heard the conversation, sighed and relaxed back onto the floor. She had so many wounds; Leni didn't know which one needed attention the most. Running to the kitchen, she flung open the drawer for a clean towel and rushed back so she could hold it over the more obvious bleeding laceration on Faith's cheek.

"Hold that, Faith. I'm going to see to Cassi. She's coming to."

Weak, suffering, her mouth swollen, Faith uttered one word. A raspy whisper she barely got out that sent shivers cascading over Leni's whole body. "Cassi?"

"She's moving Faith. Cassi's alive. I called Michael. He's on his way up and will be here in a minute. He called the ambulance. Just lay there, don't move."

Leni scooted over to where Cassi lay spread-eagled. "Cass are you okay? Do you know what happened?"

Still on the floor, Cassi balanced on her hands, arms stiff and holding her upward. She blinked away the blood that dripped down her forehead. Leni, seeing her sister's dilemma, reached over to wipe it away. "Cass, it's Leni. What happened here?"

"I-I don't know. They broke in and took Raoul."

"They who?" Leni experienced anger she'd never felt before. All-consuming, the rage filled her, making her shake from the force.

Before she could answer, Michael arrived in a swirl of masculine protection. A truck dropped from Leni's shoulders. She could hand over the reins of responsibility. Never before had she felt so useless.

Chapter Fifteen

Michael dashed into the room and came to a dead stop. "Jesus!" Leni saw his shocked face and knew how bad it looked. She just had the same experience.

"I know. That was my reaction too. When is the ambulance coming?"

Michael stopped to see Cassi beginning to recuperate on his way over to check Faith. Assuming he knew more about these sorts of injuries than she did, Leni waited and watched him gently remove the towel she'd used as a dressing for Faith. His closed expression never altered.

Stiff, professional yet caring, not the fluid, relaxed teaser she was used to, he squeezed her arm in a reassuring way before speaking. "Help should be here any minute. I have to call Trace back now. He's with Steven, having a drink in the Casino bar. I was supposed to join them until I got your call.

I cancelled, said I'd pulled a case. He'll fire me if I don't let him know what's happened here, and rightly so."

She heard it then. The deference in his tone and the flash of sympathy in his eyes before the shield returned. He used his phone and made the call, which lasted a few seconds.

"They're on their way."

"Wouldn't it have been better for them to go straight to the hospital?"

"Not the way Trace will drive. They'll be here in no time, trust me."

Leni had been rubbing Cass's back in a comforting way to keep her calm and spoke soothingly. "Honey, Trace is on his way. Don't worry. Were you hurt anywhere else besides your head?"

Though she never came out and pointedly asked, Leni worried about the baby. Cass and Trace had proudly announced their news only last week, and her health and the baby's were now a priority.

Cassi's voice sounded weak, shaky, unlike her usual husky tones that when warm, could bring men to their knees or when angry, would scare the bejesus out of them. "You called Trace?"

Michael twisted from Faith's side to answer. "I called him, Cassi. He'll be here in a few minutes. Can you tell me who did this?"

Cassi, still pale and trembly, seemed to fixate on the Taser probe suspended from her leg. She yanked at it and the light wire curled around her hand. When Michael called her name for the second time, she looked at him, appearing completely disoriented.

"Can you tell me who attacked you?"

"I don't know. A man...."

"How did they get in?"

"I opened the door for Leni." Seemingly less disoriented, she pushed the swathes of thick black hair away from her face. "I just thought it was Leni. I didn't check. He came at me."

Michael asked, "Was he carrying a pizza?"

"Yes. I think so. I remember the smell. I couldn't stop them. They took Raoul and... Oh my God, Faith."

Swivelling like a wild woman, Cassi pushed past Leni to where Faith lay still on the floor. "Faith!"

Shock had rendered the other woman silent. She lay still as a mouse frozen in fear. More than her many visible wounds, her eyes were pools of sorrow and they frightened Leni. Looking into them, one experienced a profound shock. Pity soon followed.

While Cassi inched closer to Faith, Leni saw the other probe on her side. When she went to reach for it, Michael stopped her, withdrew his phone and first took a picture to go with the many others he'd busily taken. Photos of where she'd been laying, careful to get the visual of the blood spill, her position in the room and other details that would matter to a jury.

Cassi looked at Michael, and one could see her head had cleared. Unmistakable hatred in her expression made them aware of her anger. "Look what that crazy woman did to her."

"Woman? Cassi, there was a woman here, too?"

"Oh, yeah. Crazy and mean. She did this to Faith; beat her terribly, all because Faith refused to hand over Raoul."

Before they could discuss this further, two paramedics arrived with a stretcher and close behind were Trace and Steven.

That's when all hell broke loose.

Chapter Sixteen

Steven came into the apartment behind everyone else, shouting Faith's name, rushing, pushing past the others to get to her side. Frantic, he reached out trembling hands only to pull them back, too scared to touch – too scared to inflict more pain.

Once they were able to assure him that Faith's wounds were mainly superficial, things calmed down. Examining her, the attendants insisted they needed to x-ray her jaw because of her swollen cheek, blackening eye and vicious cut, so they were preparing her for the stretcher.

Fighting through the fog of pain, Faith felt her mind clear. Aware they needed her to answer their questions; she emptied her thoughts of Raoul and turned to one of the men kneeling at her side.

Michael was gentle in his questioning. And after Trace ensured that his Cassi wasn't too badly injured, he left her with Leni and stooped beside

Faith as well.

"Can you tell us what happened here, Faith? Concentrate – from the beginning, try to remember."

While thinking back over the series of events, she voiced them. "Cassi went to let Leni in. I was holding Raoul. Then I heard scuffling and saw Cassi fighting like a warrior. She yelled for me to get him to the other room, but I couldn't. A crazy woman rushed at me and tried to drag the baby from my arms. She kept hitting me. But I wouldn't let her have him." Remembering made the sickness roil inside. Swallowing, breathing deeply, she didn't want to faint or retch, so she kept talking.

"What happened then?"

"He hit me, and I couldn't hold on any longer. I just remember Raoul screaming for me." In her agitation, she reached for Trace's hand and squeezed until he winced. "You have to find him, Trace. He needs me. You know that. He won't be happy with anyone else. We need each other." Crying hard now, she tried to swipe at her eyes so she could see his features, make sure he understood how imperative it was, not just her but for the baby.

"Shush, Faith. Don't fret." Trace spoke gently. "We're on it, and we'll get him back." Seeing the attendants were ready to set her on the stretcher, Trace leaned down and kissed her hand before letting it go. "I promise, Mike and I will do everything in our power to bring him home, okay?" His piercing stare caught hers and a message passed between them.

"Thank you."

"Steven, can I talk to you?" Trace motioned for the distraught man to follow him. Faith watched them and saw Michael and Trace surround him in the corner. When he tried to push them aside, they held him there. Leni moved to block Faith's view. It didn't help. She knew Steven's plan. Fear made her grab at Leni's arm. "Don't let Steven go vigilante. He'll get hurt. That monster will tear him to pieces."

***

Harsh, his voice no longer butter but ice, Trace stated, "You aren't leaving here, man. Faith needs you with her. Let us do our job. It's what the citizen's pay us for."

"I want to get my hands on that animal. Him and Natalie. My God, Trace! Did you see what they did? She looks like she's been in a war zone."

"And they'll pay, trust me. Right now, you can best help by answering my questions. Do you have any idea where your ex-girlfriend lives, where they might have taken Raoul?"

"Shit, no. We parted ways after Raoul was born, when she refused to be his mother. I did go after her once she'd left the hospital and tracked her to a joint she'd rented off the strip. Maybe she's there. Let's go now—"

Trace held him in place. "Not you. Faith needs you with her. Mike and I will find them. Just give us the information and let us do our jobs."

***

Cassi shook off the paramedic who'd hovered, trying to talk her into letting them take her on the stretcher and came to Faith's side. Leni stood nearby, too.

"We'll follow you to the hospital, Faith. Don't worry."

Trace moved beside her and gave his order. "Yes, Leni can go with you in the ambulance behind hers." He stared Cassi down until she capitulated.

"Shit, okay already. I'll check on you once we're there."

Leni brushed Faith's hair from her cheek. "It'll be fine, Faith. Michael and Trace will find Raoul. And Steven will stay with you."

Minutes later in the ambulance, Faith opened her eyes to see Steven's barely controlled tears. Eyes swimming in pools of regret, he never once looked away. Just continued to stare at her as he caressed the back of the hand he held gently.

"Don't worry honey, we're taking you to the hospital and they'll look after you." He reached to her face and barely touched; his gentleness comforting. The obvious grief in his voice mesmerized, making her listen carefully. "I'm so sorry, baby. Sorry I didn't pay that bitch the money she wanted. I'd never have put you and Raoul in this danger if I had any idea she'd go this far. Please forgive me."

His words rang a bell and her mind swiftly travelled to another time he'd used the same word. Not willing to go there, she zoomed back in on what he was saying now. "They'll help you feel better."

Thinking he meant the hospital, she nodded and turned her head. When she heard the soft moan he couldn't hide, she took pity on his anguish and shared her panic. "Steven. I'm scared." Allowing him to see her torment, she confessed what drove her crazy. "They took Raoul. Those crazy people took our baby. I'll never feel better until we have him back." A pressing need arose to make him understand. "I tried to fight her, but I had to protect Raoul. I wasn't strong enough to get away." Breaking down completely, she added. "I couldn't stop them. I wanted to. God knows, I tried."

"Honey, sweetheart, calm down. Look at your beautiful face and your poor body." As he spoke, he leaned over to kiss her forehead, careful not to land on any bruised area... which was difficult. "I can see how much you fought. The beating you took to save our boy shows all over your body."

"I couldn't stop her. She hit me, over and over, but I wouldn't let her touch him. She tried to grab him from my arms. I held her off. Cassi fought the man – big, mean; he hurt her. I couldn't stop him. Someone hit me, and I lost consciousness. Then you came."

"Oh baby. I'm so sorry. It had to be Natalie and her man. As I told you earlier, she'd tried to coerce me to give her more money, and I told her to get lost. I regret that now more than anything. I'd have paid her everything I own for this not to have happened."

His voice broke and that tore her to pieces. This handsome, strong businessman, charismatic and smart, cried with his head on her chest and her arms wrapped around his shoulders.

"I believe you, Steven. Don't cry. I know. They'll find him."

Righting himself, cleaning away his misery with the tissue the attendant at the back of the ambulance passed over, he agreed, "Yes, you're right. They will find him. I gave them her picture, and Trace has an 'all-points bulletin' out to every cop in the area, plus they've blasted that photo on every news channel and sent it to all the police cars in the city. They won't get far. We'll have him back soon."

Nodding, she patted his cheeks and closed her eyes. Praying was all she had left. And so, she prayed.

Chapter Seventeen

Michael and Trace headed to the address that Steven had given them, knowing it was one of the more derelict areas in the city. They'd already fed Natalie's name and birthdate on Michael's system in his police unit and were waiting to see if they got any hits for an address or phone number, anything they could use to find her tonight.

Finally, the computer finished sifting through all the programs. It came up with the same address as the apartment they'd just left, where Faith and Raoul now lived. Thankfully, it also detailed a cell phone with the number listed under Natalie Cross.

Instinctively, holding his breath, Michael started a GPS tracker working with her cell number and let out a whoosh when he hit a signal. "Got it! They're out this way but not at the same address Steven found her before. Here. It's the old apartment complex on the corner."

He pointed at a rundown building across from where Trace drove close to the curb. "Unless she left her phone behind, she's there on the third floor, corner suite, at the front."

"Good. Wanna call for backup?" Michael heard the note in Trace's voice and watched his slow grin.

He answered. "What do you think? It's two against two unless you want to count Raoul, and he'd be on our side."

"Let's go." Trace left the car and opened the trunk, reached for a Kevlar vest, handing another to Michael. He checked the rounds in his 9mm Lugar and satisfied, he fed it back into the side holster he preferred.

Once Michael had performed the same ritual, they walked together to the building.

Feeling good to have his old partner back, Michael strode to the door and opened it, no such thing as security in a building where the door looked as if it had been forced numerous times.

They made their way to the stairs and as soon as they hit the third-floor landing, Trace signalled for Michael to halt and listen. They both chuckled when they heard a baby screaming. Suddenly Trace's cell vibrated to let him know a call came through.

"McGuire here." Michael watched Trace's face cloud over and fear struck. *What now?*

"Okay. You did right. We're moving in on them as I speak."

Trace listened and soon grinned into the phone. "Because I can hear Raoul giving them hell. He's howling louder than a tomcat with his nuts caught in a trap. We'll be there soon."

Michael couldn't help himself. "What happened?"

"Steven got the call. They want to trade, cash for the baby."

"Figures. Some people shouldn't be allowed to walk free."

"No Kidding. We'll be changing that status right now. How do you want to play this? He has a Taser, we know that. But does he have a gun? We can't take any chances with Raoul."

"I know. So, busting in—"

Before Mike could finish his sentence and decide on their strategy, the door opened, and a man burst out. Slamming it behind him, he was cussing about fucking women and screaming brats.

Trace stepped forward, pulled out his badge and snarled. "Stop right there, asshole. LVMPD."

Shoving Trace aside, the perp tried to flee but didn't get far. Though a big guy, Trace could move like greased lightning if need be. He had the baby thief against the wall in seconds. Not finished by a long shot, the idiot threw the first punch.

Trace skipped out of the way and countered. It struck the other man's arm but did nothing to slow him down. Next, he tried aiming at Trace's midriff only to have Trace twist, so it ended up hitting his side. On a roll, he tried again, only this time, Trace's fist hit the solar plexus and he went down.

Michael, not waiting to see the outcome of the fight, tried the door and used his shoulder to burst through. His sudden appearance startled the woman bending over the baby. Frantic, she picked him up, staggering, holding the screaming kid in front of her as he approached. He lifted his empty hands, hoping to calm her down.

"Don't come near me." Confused, high from her latest hit, she clutched a distraught Raoul next to her chest. The poor baby's arms were flailing, and his head flopped dangerously from side to side. He wore nothing but a soiled diaper and a tiny white shirt that contrasted brightly against the redness in his face.

Before Michael could negotiate, the woman ran through the open blinds to the balcony.

He had no idea of her plans, but the hair on the back of his neck began to signal wildly. *She's lost it. And she has Raoul.*

Following carefully, he took a few moments to remove his jacket, whip his tie over his head and undo a few shirt buttons. Then he stuck his gun behind him in his belt and rolled up his sleeves. Within seconds he'd joined her outside and found her balanced on the black iron balcony railing, one leg already over.

"Hey honey, what's wrong with your baby?"

She looked at him unable to believe what stood

in front of her eyes.

"Who're you? Are you a cop?"

He chuckled as if amused. "I'm a neighbor. I heard your baby crying, and hoped I could help. I have a couple kids of my own, and I know how to soothe them when they get to crying so hysterically."

As if Raoul understood, he ramped up his angry, shrill screams. His vehement complaints rang in the dark of the hot, sultry night.

Natalie, dazed, uncomprehending, cradled the baby awkwardly. "He's mine. I have to go now. He's hungry." Then she put her other leg over the balcony.

Michael, sweating bullets, inched closer. "Don't go that way, neighbor. You'll fall and hurt the little guy. You don't want to hurt him, now do you?"

As if affronted, Natalie shook her head. "No. I'd never do that. But he has to come with me."

"Why? I can look after him. Let me take him and see if I can quiet the poor fellow down."

Michael held his breath. From the corner of his eye he saw Trace waiting, not moving, scared to let her see him and get spooked even worse. Her hold on Raoul was precarious to say the least, and if she let go, he'd hurtle to the ground. Suddenly, Trace disappeared, and Michael knew he'd most likely gone to call backup.

Ripping through the silence of the night, Raoul had reached such a pitch that his distress had broken boundaries from him being angry to uncontrollable. Michael's heart hurt for the wretched little soul.

Before he could say another word, Natalie stepped so close to the edge that all he could do was grab for her arms. As he did so, she dropped the child.

Chapter
Eighteen

While she whispered prayer after prayer, telling whoever listened she'd do whatever he asked of her if only he'd let Raoul come home, Faith's face had been stitched and x-rayed and the nurses had dealt with her other wounds.

Cassi had been examined as well and both girls were considered lucky. But they were advised to remain overnight in case of concussion.

When Cassi'd shown up wearing a green hospital gown and looking like her old self, Faith had been afraid to ask Cass about her own baby. But Leni had no such reservations. As soon as Cassi entered Faith's room, Leni jumped up and groaned, "Well?"

Cassi grinned. Her face wreathed in smiles told its own story. "What a worrier you are. The baby is fine. Being tased didn't bother him whatsoever. Thank goodness. But it sure as hell made me take notice. Hurt like all get-out."

Steven had left earlier to take a call, and he re-entered the room to return to his post, the chair closest to Faith. His hand searched for hers.

Being supportive, Leni had taken up her position in the chair on the other side, so Cassi slumped across the foot of the bed.

"Have you heard anything at all?" She searched their faces, and Faith saw the worry she felt for her nephew.

Steven answered; his voice shaky. "They think they've found them. I don't want to get your hopes up too high in case it's a false alarm, but they're closing in right now, so we should hear something soon."

Faith's pain had gone way past tears. It had buried itself so deep in her soul that the rest of her days would be spent yearning to hold the lost child. To shower him with kisses and love him so hard, he'd never be afraid again.

How she knew his state, she had no idea. But she sensed his fear, his anger, crying, needing her... wanting her arms around him to keep him safe. No one could tell her different. The link she felt to Raoul was as strong a connection as someone using a phone for the first time. They didn't have a clue of how it worked, it just did. She heard him crying... she couldn't shut it off.

Suddenly the door to her room opened and Trace stepped in first. He held the door and

Michael followed with a whimpering, crying little bundle in his big arms.

Faith almost fell out of the bed in her rush to get to the child. "Raoul!"

Her own arms, held in front, were shaking with tension and excitement. "My God, you found him. Shush baby, Faith's got you now." She crushed him to her chest and spread kisses all over his red, angry face, nuzzling him, cuddling him close and then holding him away so both her and Steven could see the baby.

Steven's hand shook as he caressed Raoul's head gently. Bending, he kissed the little forehead and then the tiny, waving hand.

***

Within seconds, Raoul quieted, sighed and promptly fell asleep. Faith, Leni and Cassi all cooed and fussed over him while Steven held his hand out to Michael and forced a man hug. "Thank you, Michael. For bringing him home. I'll never forget it. Anything! Anytime! If it's in my power, it's yours."

Touched and not afraid to show his emotion, Michael nodded, hugged back and added, "Just so you know, I wasn't the one who caught the baby when your old girlfriend accidently dropped him over a balcony. I can tell you, I was never so scared in all my life. But Trace had enough instinct to stand below just in case. When Natalie dropped Raoul, he caught him. Most beautiful thing I ever saw. So, if you want to thank anyone, man. It's that guy."

Steven turned to Trace, now wrapped around Cassi, beaming at her great news about their baby. Steven put an arm around them both. "I take it all's well with your world."

Cassi answered. "Yes. And now that Raoul is home, it couldn't be better. I'm so happy for you and Faith that it all turned out."

"Thanks to your husband. Michael just told me that he saved Raoul from a fall, and I can't begin to tell you—"

Trace held up his hand to stop the speech, and said, "I'm glad it all turned out fine. He's my family now too, my nephew, and I want what's best for the little man."

Cassi, flushed with pride, took Trace's hand and led him to the door. "Let's leave these two alone now and go to my room so you can tell me all about what happened." Trace's obvious agreement made Steven chuckle as he witnessed his friend all but drag her from the room.

Meanwhile, Michael went over to Faith to gather her and the child in a hug that Leni soon joined in on. Steven's heart swelled when he witnessed their obvious love for his nanny. Pride filled him to where he almost choked from the overflow.

What a lucky man I am!

Arm in arm, Michael and Leni wished them goodnight, and they too left the room. Now only his sleeping baby and his Faith remained.

He removed his shoes first and next his jacket. Then he lowered the lights and made his way to the opposite side of the bed where Faith had Raoul nestled close.

Lying down beside her, he gathered them both into his arms and laid his cheek on the top of her head. Unable to stop himself, he kissed her hair, breathing in the flowery yet spicy scent she used. So far, he'd gotten no resistance and that gave him the nerve to say what had to be said.

"Forgive me,' he whispered.

He felt her stiffen, and he tightened his hold gently.

"Me, forgive you? I don't understand."

"I've been a blind fool, Faith... my beautiful sunshine. You've given me more joy, made me feel more loved than any time in my whole life. I respectfully accept whatever you've done in the past that made you into the wonderful person you are today. If you ever want to share those experiences, I'll be honored to listen. If not, we'll move on. What I do know is this. Any woman who'd let herself be brutally beaten to save a child, is the woman I want – no, need – in my life, as my wife and the mother of our children."

After his speech, Steven held his breath, praying his earlier stupidity hadn't driven her so far away that she wouldn't trust him now.

Chapter Nineteen

Faith stiffened when she realized Steven's intentions. He was slipping onto the bed beside her, hugging her, kissing her hair. What had happened?

Afraid to ask him, she just accepted his ministrations. His gentleness charmed her, and half of her soul flew from her body to nestle inside of his. Never again would she love another man. He was her mate.

He spoke, and she listened. And when he said what every woman yearns to hear, she knew firsthand what heaven must feel like.

"Will you marry me, Faith?"

Beautiful words spoken in a voice not quite confident had joy zinging through her. Too overcome, she nodded.

"I need to hear you say the words, Faith. Tell me you love me the way I love you and that we'll be husband and wife – happy forever. You, me and Raoul."

She stuttered, a habit she'd thought she'd lost years before. "I-I want to so much, Steven. But are you sure you can accept all my baggage." Not knowing how else to warn him, she felt it only fair to give him his last chance of escape.

"I've never been more sure of anything else in my life. The blinders have come off, honey. I see you clearly. And I want you."

"What about Raoul? What if he should find out about my past?"

"He won't care. Our little wise man recognized your heart of gold right from the beginning. It just took this blind fool a bit longer to see you for the angel you are. Faith, please..."

Unable to listen to his worried tones, knowing he suffered, waiting for her answer, she said, "Then I'd be happy to marry you."

Soon, her face radiant from his warm kisses, proving how precious she was, he added, chuckling, "I just had a thought. I'm so happy; I want everyone I care about to feel this way. Maybe you can make sure that Leni gets your wedding bouquet next so we can pass on this happiness to her and Michael."

She giggled happily. "I'll do my best."

The End

Leni

Her Sweet Revenge Series – Book #6
By
Mimi Barbour

NYT & USA Today Best-selling author

~*~*~

Leni Santino's happy life turns upside down from five words uttered carelessly. "Sergio Mandalas killed your cousin." Stunned speechless, her heart closes and the hard facade she'd worn in the past returns. Everything she loves becomes meaningless.

Since her wonderful cousin, Mani, the man who gave up his future for her, died senselessly, how can she carry on knowing his killer walks free?

When her long-lost mother, a woman she'd never met, appears to warn her that a blackmailer has found out the family secret, everything spins unbearably out of control.

Detective Mike Kowalski loves the spirited boxing chick in every way a man can idolize his woman. But he feels her slipping away. With the help of their friends, he tries to keep her safe. In the end, the choices are hers to make. All he can do is stand by and watch...

And be ready to pick up the pieces.

Chapter One

"He killed my cousin Mani! Sergio Mandalas? Are you sure, Flossie?" Leni Santino felt like a pile driver had plunged into her stomach. "How do you know?"

"I saw him at your sister Cassi's wedding. Remember how he stayed in the background with that Doug guy who worked for Dani at the Lipstick Club? Of course, before we found out Doug was a spy for Mandalas. I knew him enough to approach and say hello. That's when I saw Sergio's hand holding his beer. His fingers are tattooed. The night the *Soldados* shot up the club, I was delivering drinks to Mani's table on the window side and saw the shooter's hands. They were tattooed in the same way. After the bullets had stopped, and Mani lay dead, that image became engraved in my brain. I told the cops that night, but nothing ever happened."

Suddenly, Leni slammed down the coffee mug she'd been holding. "Does Cass know? Did she see him?"

"Gosh, Leni. Everything happened so fast that night, I doubt it. She was too busy hauling Dani's ass out of her chair and protecting her."

"Without a doubt, you know it was the *Soldados* gang who were responsible for the incident, right?"

"Oh, sure. We were told it was in retaliation for a hit on one of Mandala's men. A couple of Dani's hopped-up idiots killed his two little girls in a house drive-by. Didn't you hear about that? The bunch of us who worked at the joint were sickened by the incident. But we never suspected that they'd attack the club. Dumb really, because it was reasonable to expect some sort of revenge."

Leni lifted her hands to push her long hair away from her face and realized they were shaking. In fact, her whole body had undergone a shocking transition from a happy, newly engaged girl to one with a disgusting, grinning monkey on her back. Floored, sickened, she didn't know how to react, how she should feel.

When the steel started to form in her heart, and the disgust and horror began to build in her mind, she knew she was in trouble.

How could she just let the man walk free after he killed the one person in her life who'd loved her enough to die for her? Mani had given up his future to save Leni. Smarter than most, he'd forced his way to the top of the *Armas Jóvenes,* Young Guns gang, so he could secure her freedom.

A teen runaway from a family who'd done well by her, spoiled and full of herself, Leni'd left the only home she'd ever known. Took off in a huff one night and never came back. Filled with self-righteous indignation because, though adored by her Uncle Phil and cousin Mani, her Aunt Barb often gave her a hard time. Sick of feeling like a second-class family member, she'd headed straight from security to life on the streets.

The fact that her own mother had abandoned her as a small baby, leaving her in the care of her brother's family, had affected her from the day she'd understood what happened. As a little girl, she'd waited for her mother to return, to come and get her so they could be together. Many times she'd look at the photo of her beautiful parent and dream that she'd return and beg for her forgiveness. But it never happened. Using this as the excuse she needed to bolt, she did and ended up getting herself in a lot of trouble.

Befriended by a sicko known as Juan Acedo, following him into a local gang called the *Armas Jóvenes,* she'd sunk lower than she'd ever wanted to. Gang life was hard, it mostly disgusted her and eventually, so did Juan. Then Mani had found her, and things changed.

Understanding that no one is ever allowed to break away once they're a member, he'd made it happen for her by joining the same gang and becoming second-in-command to the leader, Dani Andino. Once the boss worked with him and realized his genius, she'd made the deal, and Leni, Arlene to those who knew her then, had walked.

Right into a local gym where she'd found a reason for living. Happiness for her was putting on a pair of boxing gloves, climbing into the ring and facing a challenge.

Today, US Featherweight champion, she felt on top of the world. Then she remembered a saying her aunt used about her own personal business associates during the time when they weren't getting along. *Oh, how the mighty have fallen.*

She'd always known she'd get pushed off her pedestal by another woman – younger, stronger and hungrier than herself – but she never thought a nightmare from her past would be the reason for her defeat. Sitting in the fancy restaurant across from Flossie, she'd hit the ditch and lay there wallowing in a sticky pool of remorse.

Life as she knew it – the happy woman who'd entered the place to meet an old friend – had vanished. In her place was a hardened, empty shell of that girl. Internally fragmented, all she had in her mind was how she could get close enough to kill Sergio Mandalas without anyone ever having to find out. Especially her baldheaded, green-eyed fiancé, Detective Michael Kowalski.

Chapter Two

After lunch, Leni went back to the gym where she worked out with her sparring partner, Adam. Rusty, her manager, the old man she adored, who'd been instrumental in her success, stood at the side of the ring. After pounding on the ropes a few times, agitation on his craggy features, he bellowed, "Leni, quit trying to kill the man. He's there to help you train, not get the shit kicked outta him from your pissy mood. You and Michael have a spat or sumpthin?"

"You want me in good shape for my next bout, leave me the fuck alone."

"Okay! That's it. Adam, work with the boys, Jack wanted your help. Leni, in my office. Pronto. And don't give me any sass lady. We need to talk."

Five minutes later, Leni, with the hood of her sweatshirt shading her face, slouched on the small sofa in Rusty's postage stamp office where files, posters and the clutter of a messy man took up most of the space.

"Jesus, Rusty, how the hell can you work in here? Look at the shit you have all over. Your desk's under there somewhere, right?"

"Hey, don't start on me. You've got a tick up your ass, and I want to know what it is."

"Tick up my ass. You never talk like that around Cass. Just me. Why's that?"

"'Cause, I've known Cass since she spit her baby cereal all over me, and it's become a habit to mind my manners around her. Plus, she doesn't cuss the way you do, and quit changing the subject. Something's up, brat. What is it?" His tuke being mauled by his gnarly old hands as he leaned against the edge of his desk was evidence that she'd gotten to him.

This was the room where she'd brought him the proof from her mother's old diary that she was Cassi Santino's half sister. That her mother, the woman who'd disappeared from her life after she was born, never to be heard from since, had been in love with José Santino and gotten pregnant. Being only eighteen and scared of her parents, she'd had the baby, dropped it off at her brother Phil's house and left town.

"You got another title match coming up, missy. It's gonna be a tough fight. I need you focused. So, tell old Rusty who pissed in your corn flakes this morning and we'll deal. Clear it up and get your head back in the ring."

Leni stared at Rusty and saw concern shining

back at her. His blue eyes, one totally blind, held a softness that she knew most others never saw. She mattered to him, and that fact mattered to her.

Yet, how the hell does one explain that her heart's been mangled from a story she wished she'd never heard? The man who killed her cousin led one of the most notorious gangs in Las Vegas. She'd never get close enough to exact revenge. Not unless she used Cassi, and that would put her sister in jeopardy.

With her muddled mind flipping from one scenario to another, she decided that she needed to fob Rusty off with a bogus explanation that would get her ejected from the hot seat. Her biggest fault, wearing her feelings out front, needed to stop. If she was going to pull off the plan her mind had begun forming, she'd have to keep those emotions under wraps.

"I'm just in a bad mood, Rusty. You know Michael's been trying to find my mother for me, right?"

Rusty nodded. "Which is a piss-poor idea if you ask me. She cut you out of her life, so why should you let her back in now? Chances are the broad changed her name, has a new life and doesn't want to be found."

"Or she died. I want to know either way. Not that I'll approach her. That's not the issue here. I just want to know. And Mike's seen it bugging me and has promised to find out what he can."

"That man's so goofy over you, he'd give you the moon if he could. So, why're you bitchy?"

"Because his search is going nowhere. Every lead has been a dead end. He called me earlier to say that his last investigation had ended up a false trail."

"So, let it go. That's what's going to get the shit kicked outta ya if'n you don't. You need to clear your mind and focus on the battle facing you in the ring. Charo Hall is good, Leni. In fact, she's more than good. She has a God-given talent. Her footwork, weaving and punches have a synchronicity that all talented fighters strive for. Plus, the ability to battle hard yet not take a beating from her opponents."

Sitting up, taking notice, Leni said, "That sounds like me you're describing."

"Yep, it's what takes you from being a good boxer to remarkable. And why I put up with your shitty attitude."

Laughing now, Leni's normal good humor flooded back. Uplifted, she did what came hard to her and stood down. "Yeah, I'm a handful. Sorry, coach-of-the-year." She hugged Rusty's arm on her way to the door and laughed when he grouchily smacked at her hands.

"Behave, brat. Go hang out with Cassi for a while or Faith and get your head on straight. Your sister promised to work out with you and Adam tomorrow, and she'll put you through your paces.

Hell, if you think I'm riding you, you ain't seen nothing yet."

"Hey, no kidding, she's even tougher than you, and I'd have said that's impossible."

"She can't stand seeing you get beat, kid. It breaks her up."

"She's not the only one." She opened the door and turned for her parting shot. "Michael has to handcuff himself to his seat so he doesn't jump into my fights.'

Chapter Three

Taking Rusty's advice, Leni drove to the *Little and Delgado's* law office. Once there, she worked on the secretary, Doris.

"Any chance to see Cass for a few minutes. And before you ride my ass, no I don't have an appointment."

Doris, a middle-aged blonde who didn't scare easy looked up, and as soon as she saw who was in front of her desk, she changed from grumpy to a packet of Splenda.

"Aw, sure Leni. I'll ring her phone." As she punched in the numbers, she smiled, making her face almost scary. Her attitude had done a hundred and eighty degree switch from gorilla to cutesy chimp when she'd found out that Leni was not only Cass's sister but the US Featherweight champion.

"How's the training going for your fight next

weekend?"

"I'm in good shape. Rusty stays on top of me, and Cass never lets up."

"So you know, I've already bought my ticket and will be there to cheer you on."

"Thanks, Doris. How sweet." Even though Leni was reacting using her professional persona, a slice of delight slivered through her. It gratified her to think that her talent could affect someone like Doris – a lot of Doris's – male and female alike. All the training, the aches, the painful recoveries, and the constant striving to make her body go further, be stronger, work harder suddenly had incentive. Although, if she was honest with herself, there was a deeper, more insidious reason for her need to fight.

Not totally understanding but knowing that an insidious hunger and a deeply buried anger drove her, kept her mean enough to turn into a machine in the ring, she saw it clearly in herself. Yet her sister, who if she was honest, could be even better than she was, had no desire at all to compete. Having been trained by their brother, Raoul, she'd always enjoyed the challenge. It had never become the pivot of her happiness. The need that drove Leni was missing in Cassi. But what she had in spades was the instincts, the love of the dance. It's what Leni strove for every time she worked out with Cass. To her, boxing was deadly serious. To Cass it was fun.

"Hey little sister." Cass approached with the hug that Leni had finally become used to accepting and even sharing.

"Hi, Cass. Do you have a minute?"

"For you, always. Come into the office. Maria's off on a case so we have the place to ourselves."

"I noticed that the wording on the window has changed and the office is now known as *Little and Delgado*. Has Mr. Sampson finally retired?"

"He has, and he let Maria buy his shares so she's now a full partner." Cass grinned in a furtive manner, leaned closer to Leni and whispered, "Gus Little has already intimated that as soon as I get my law degree, he'll be ready to sell me his shares in the office leaving Maria and I as full partners. I'm ecstatic."

"Okay, now that is good news, Cass. I'm proud of you. I know it's hard with you being pregnant, helping me at the gym and still a newlywed, but you seem to love the law classes you've started."

In the office now with the door closed, both girls relaxing in the chairs by the desk, Cass admitted, "I've never been so happy, Leni. Truthfully, it scares me. I keep waiting for something to rock my world."

"How's Trace liking his position as police chief? Mike says he's a born leader and the others would follow him to hell and back as long as he asked them to go there with him."

Cass grinned; her black hair that now reached

her shoulders formed a curly mass around her face. She pushed it back behind her ears and sighed. "I'd follow him to hell, too. He has a way about him where a person feels instantly protected. Like he could move any mountain... turn wrong to right. His mother taught him well."

Leni felt Cass's eyes on her and knew a question she couldn't answer would follow, but then like it happened often with Cass, she got a surprise.

"You and Mike want to come for supper tonight and watch the fights on TV?"

Chapter Four

Mike Kowalski got home earlier than normal and sensed immediately that something had changed his happy little fiancée back into a woman he recognized from the past. He hadn't liked that hard-hearted person very much, even though he recognized – had always recognized – that this girl was his life partner.

He swept her into his arms and rather than wind around him like she had done most previous days, she stiffened. Hoping to bring back his girl, he asked, "Hey, baby. How's your day been?"

"Okay. You?"

"Good. Until now. What's up?"

She backed away and wouldn't look at him. Incensed, she shot back, "Why would you ask me that?"

He took her arms gently, forced her to face him and then lifted her chin so she had to look him in the eye. "Because I love you. Because something's wrong. And because you need to tell me what's happened before I go crazy. Do you need more reasons?"

Yanking herself from his gentle hold, she pushed his reaching hands away and stepped back. "You're crazy. There's nothing wrong with me except for having to deal with a paranoid boyfriend who's on my case. Cass asked us over for supper tonight. Do you want to go?"

Worried, Mike decided instantly. "Sure, let's go and enjoy ourselves. Maybe a night out will be good for us. We've stuck close to home for a while now." The reason was after being apart all day, when he'd arrive home, they'd be at each other, in bed, making love. By the time they finally got around to cooking dinner, it was always too late to go out.

Within a short while, they were headed to Cass and Trace's house, the silence in the car so not the norm. Unknown to others, Leni loved to ramp up their pre-loaded music and most times would sing along, her voice surprisingly good. He loved to just drive, listen to her sing and thank the Lord they'd found each other.

Tonight, the quiet was deadly. He pulled into a gas station to fill his tank, and as his custom, he perused the area. Suddenly, he spotted something that didn't sit well with him. A couple were having a fight in the parking lot. The small blonde clutched her purse to her chest while a fat son of a bitch was determined to get it from her. Two kids in the car were crying while the third, an older boy, had decided to come to his mother's rescue.

"Dad, let her go. It's her wages, and we need the money for rent and food." About ten or maybe even younger, the boy tried to get between his mother and her attacker, even though he looked scared to death and flinched from fists he knew would come his way. Pushing the boy roughly aside, the man doubled his efforts. "Give me the bag, Millie. I want the money."

That's when Mike noticed two other losers waiting in the background, watching, grinning, uncaring... not a beating heart between them.

He bent to the open window to let Leni know he was calling for backup, and she needed to stay in the car. Except she wasn't there. Instead, she was making it her business to interfere with a potential battle.

Jesus!

He quickly rehung the gas hose, used his cellphone to get a squad car and followed.

Chapter Five

Leni couldn't believe that a father could act like a lunatic towards his wife and in front of his kids. He must be high or drunk. She approached with the intention of talking sense into the asshole. Except she didn't see his two friends waiting in the background.

She used her indoor voice, speaking low, "Hey, man. Let her go. She doesn't want to give you her money, and I don't blame her. Those kids need it a lot more than you do."

Badass dad never let go of the handbag, but his hand came toward Leni, his finger pointing, rage written all over his sweaty face. "Back off, bitch. No one asked you to interfere. This is between me and my wife." This time he used his hand to grab at the poor woman's hair, and he twisted her head awkwardly, hurting her.

Before Leni could stop him, two men approached, one on each side. They intimidated by getting too close. "Yeah, bitch. Stay out of it."

She saw what they missed. The young boy had grabbed a huge stick and was swinging it to hit his father. If he connected, all hell would break loose. She also saw Mike approach, his swagger distinctive. He grabbed the end of the stick before it reached the intended subject and pulled it from the boy's hand, but he didn't let it go.

Showing the badge attached to his gun holster, he said, "Detective Mike Kowalski from the Las Vegas Police Department. What's the problem here?" Mike glared at the two men who hadn't backed off. He took a threatening step toward them, the stick held firmly.

"Thank God you came. My husband knows its payday, and he's come to steal my wages. But we'll be evicted if I don't pay the rent this month, and I have three kids who need a roof over their heads. We have to buy food, and shithead here wants the money to stick up his ugly nose, him and the two gorillas he came with."

Obviously finding courage now that help had arrived, the mom yanked her purse from hands suddenly limp and motioned for her son to get back into the car. Then she turned to Mike. "Can you arrest him, stick him in a cell for twenty-four hours until whatever shit he's taken wears off?"

"We can if you press assault charges, ma'am."

"He never touched her. I saw it all. He grabbed the purse is all." The taller lanky watcher pitched in with his two cents.

Leni, unable to keep silent, added, "What about you two coming at me? An innocent bystander."

"We never laid a hand on you, lady."

Seeing his chance at getting the money failing, badass made one last bid. "Millie, honey, I'll get work tomorrow and pay you back, but I need that money tonight. I'm sick. I'm in pain. I need some medication." He lunged at her.

Maybe because she had someone else in her corner, or maybe the woman had hit the end of her victim persona, whatever drove her to attack, no one could say. But attack she did. Throwing her purse into the open window of the car, nails ready, she lunged at the sicko who'd fathered her kids. She scratched, hit, pulled hair and pounded his body, all the while screaming curses and letting go of her wall of frustrations.

"You wicked, sad excuse of a man, I hate what you've become, what you've done to yourself. You're not sick, you're higher than you've ever been before. The pain in your back is long gone but your hunger for the drugs has made you dependent. I never, ever want to see you around me and the kids again. Eat shit and die you bastard."

Cowering, protecting himself, the sniveling father took the punishment for a short while, but when he'd reached his limit, he hauled back his fist. That's when Mike stepped in and grabbed his arm. Within a few seconds, Mike had him on the ground, face planted in the dust.

Smiling, Leni loved watching the play unwinding in front of her. That is until one of the losers beside her saw his friend being taken down by the cop and started to interfere. He dove at Mike and before he connected, she'd tripped him up and swirling in a circle, full force behind her backhand, she connected, and the loser went down for the count. Lanky, his buddy, faded into the night not to be seen again.

Pissed, Mike yelled, "What the hell do you think you're doing?"

"Just helping my man." She held her hands up in front of her showing she'd finished.

The sirens that had been in the distance sounded louder and seconds later, two squad cars squealed to a stop in the lot.

Chapter Six

Once they arrived at Cass's small home, Leni spoke before Mike, her voice filled with excitement. "Sorry we're late but we just got involved in a family dispute at the gas station. It took a while to give our statements."

Trace, Cass's husband, the Las Vegas Police Chief who happened to be Mike's boss, spoke, his tone serious, "Anyone injured?"

Mike, still annoyed at Leni for putting herself in danger and getting involved with something that was police business, answered, "Just a poor bastard hooked on some shit who'd decided his family didn't need the wife's wages as much as he needed his special kind of medication. Oh yeah, and a stupid dude who thought to interfere before Leni dissuaded him. Nothing serious."

Head shaking, disgust showing, Trace admitted, "We get so many of those cases, it makes me sick – sick and sad. Many of the people hooked on opioids today were upstanding citizens just trying to find help for an injury or a pain too harsh to live with. Bastard doctors were quick to dispense those pills and now look at the result – broken lives full of broken people."

Leni spoke up, "My sympathy fades when a big man tries to overpower his smaller wife to steal her money."

Mike added, "And my sympathy fades when my girl thinks she can interfere with a situation that needs a cop with training." He was still pissed at Leni walking into danger the way she'd done. Hell, those kinds of creeps often carried and weren't scared to pull the gun and use it. Hopped up on shit, who knew what they were capable of.

Twisting, quick as a wink, she came back at him. "Just because I don't wear a badge, doesn't mean I can't look after myself. The last time I cowered in front of a maniac, I needed Faith to step in and save me. Never again. I might not be a fucking cop, but I am trained."

Mike saw Trace and Cass share a look and knew they'd just noticed the change in Leni. Then he wasn't wrong. She'd reverted to the girl he'd first met, the one with a chip on her shoulder the size of the Empire State Building.

***

Cass pulled Mike aside in the kitchen where they were getting the dessert. "What's going on? She's worse than when I first met her. Jumpy, full of anger. I thought she'd left all that behind her. And did you notice how often she brought up Mani tonight? I know she loved her cousin dearly, but it's like he died yesterday, and it's been nearly a year."

Mike leaned against the counter. His right hand rubbed at his bald head, something he did when perplexed or needing a moment. Then he crossed his arms as if to stop from sharing too much. But his words were revealing, and he knew Cass picked up on his angst. "So, it's not just me."

She approached and gently rubbed his arm. "It's probably nothing, Mike. She goes through these periods from time to time and works things out. If you want, I can talk to her, but it could just be she's fretting about the fight coming up. Charo Hall is a good fighter; strong, deadly as cancer and lethal if one doesn't take her threat seriously."

He perked up and drilled questions, forgetting he wasn't at work. "Leni's good enough, Cass, right? She's trained for the fight? She can win? Tell me she can win."

"Of course, she can win. I wouldn't be working with her to get her ready if I thought she had no chance. Neither would Rusty, and he's a boxing genius any fighter would be fortunate to train with."

"That's what I thought." Back to rubbing his head, he shyly added, "I'm hoping when we get married, she'll decide the fight game isn't for her anymore. Instead she'll maybe think of starting a family." He glanced at her big belly and added,

"How're you and Trace Junior doing?"

Cassi laughed and patted her belly. Then she quickly took Mike's hand and held it over where the baby was kicking up a storm. "I figure Junior's already in training."

Mike's features broke up and his eyes filled. Sentimental to a fault, the big guy wore his heart on his sleeve. "Now isn't this just the best miracle in God's handbag."

A silly grin on his face, Mike turned to see Leni watching from the hallway. He saw Cass reach out her hand and was thrilled when Leni approached and held on. Then she put Leni's hand on her stomach beside his, and he saw the wonder appear on Leni's face.

Seeing her like this, he fell in love all over again. Now there's his girl.

***

That night, Leni let go of the hate she'd been harboring for Sergio and reveled in the soft, warm emotions that touching Cass's stomach had initiated. Mike seemed to sense she'd reverted, and as soon as they arrived at their modern apartment, he'd gotten glasses of wine, turned on their favorite music and swung her into his arms.

Slow dancing, hips grinding while his lips traveled everywhere on her face, her neck, into the top of her blouse, she thrilled at his way of loving. Letting herself enjoy the sexy treatment, the feeling of being adored like only a man with a big heart knew how to do, she kept her head together and her recent thoughts closed off.

His kisses stirred her in the same way they always had the power to do. Eyes closed, lost to the thrill, she opened her lips and let him invade her mouth, loving the ravenous hunger he aroused. Angling in as close as humanly possible, her moans as loud as his, she strained to keep his wandering lips on hers.

Unable to keep their hands from searching and caressing, he lowered her to the floor and got serious.

That's about the same time his phone rang.

Chapter Seven

Leni had offered to stay with Cass as one of her delivery room buddies along with Faith who'd promised to be there also. Now, she dithered about this responsibility. Knowing herself and how she hated seeing anyone she loved in pain, she fretted that when Cass needed her the most, she'd totally fizz out and be useless.

Meeting Faith in the maternity ward, she asked, "Have you seen her yet?" Leni's voice shook and her freezing hands wouldn't stop shaking. "Man, you'd think it was me giving birth, I'm so nervous."

"I know. Me, too. Steve's been trying to talk me down ever since we left the fight. By the way, you were awesome up there tonight. I don't think I've ever seen you like that before. It was like you were in a zone. Like someone else had taken over your body."

"I know. It scared me, Faith. I was on autopilot.

Seriously, I didn't feel anything." She couldn't share with Faith how unmitigated, disgusting hate had consumed her and not for the other fighter. If this was the way Cassi had felt about her twin brother, Raoul's killer, she now understood the powerful force that drove her to get that person and make them pay. Her thoughts stopped there, and a huge wash of disgust filled her, an emotion she'd thought she'd previously dealt with.

Soon, Faith on one side of Cass and Leni on the other, they conversed and yattered like they were at a social gathering. "So, where's all this pain you're supposed to be going through? It looks like a piece of cake from where I'm standing," Leni teased her half-sister and got a grin in reply.

"Doc says I'm dilated more than halfway. I would think things should be starting soon. Where's Trace?"

"You've asked that four times in the last ten minutes. Remember, he had to go because of the shooting on the strip by Caesar's. He'd never have left you, but there were multiple deaths and a lot of injuries. Both he and Mike were called... remember?"

"Yeah, yeah. I remember. You don't have to shove it down my throat. I'm pregnant, not suffering from Alzheimer's."

Oh! Oh! Leni watched Faith's expression and knew she'd seen it too. They were in for a long night. She turned to Cassi and said, "Sorry, sis.

Can I get you anything?"

"Yeah, get me some fucking painkillers, 'cause ladies, Junior's getting ready to meet his family. Oh my God, owww..."

Chapter Eight

Mike watched Trace working through the night, his phone in his hand constantly while he checked with either Faith or Leni at the hospital. The bastard who'd gone on the shooting rampage earlier had escaped and was still at large. Mind you, if their last information was correct, thanks to Mandalas, he and his gang had the shooter corralled at the old potato chip factory on the edge of town.

On their way there now, Mike asked for an update. "What's going on at the hospital?"

"Faith said Cassi's in active labor. Up till now, it's been easy, she's breathed through most of the pains and they've been far enough apart that she was getting breaks in-between. Then she said something strange – especially from Faith."

"What's that?"

"She told me I wasn't to let Cassi get anywhere

near my gun."

Mike laughed, remembering some of the stories he'd heard from his sisters and mom when they talked girl talk about their deliveries. Nah! Warning Trace wouldn't help. He decided to keep his mouth shut on that subject. Instead, he said, "Jesus, I hope we get this asshole soon. Mandalas and his guys have him cornered, right?"

"That's what he told me. They've cornered the prick at the old factory buildings and forced him into the office area."

"Crissakes, what's this world coming to when the Vegas Police Department has to depend on the hottest gang in town to catch a killer?" Mike watched the streets whiz past, in awe at how Trace handled the speeding vehicle.

"I know, hey? It's fucking lunacy. The man's a thieving seller of drugs and prostitution; he should be in a cell. Yet here we are working with him, and it's not for the first time. It's hard to explain but the man's got a code."

"He's a strange one alright."

"Saved my ass in the past." Trace wheeled the black SUV around another corner and had Mike holding on to the dash. "Cassi won't hear anyone badmouth him. She's stoic when it comes to her friends, and she considers him a special one. Goes back to the time when she was after Raoul's killer. Sergio was there for her, more than once."

"He's got my vote. If he helps us get this maniac

off the streets tonight, I'll buy him a beer any day."

They pulled into the derelict area, the field around the darkened factory yard in total disrepair. Staying back behind the fence, they left their car and headed toward where four other men were waiting. Backup was on the way, so they had a few minutes before the SWAT team arrived.

Sergio stepped out from behind his bodyguard and approached. "How's Cass?"

"Faith says her labor is getting harder."

"Fuck! I feel for her. But after tonight she'll be a Mama Bear, and there'll be no one better."

Trace smiled. "Yeah, I know. I just need to get to her, and this asshole is keeping me away. We gotta bring him in now. I don't have time to mess around. The others are on their way. You know for sure he hasn't slipped out the back?"

"My boys have every window and exit covered. He's inside and going nowhere. Bastard should just do us all a favor and shoot himself." Sergio's voice registered the truth he believed.

"Not this fool. Before the night is out, he's looking forward to taking as many more with him as he can. What's he got to lose?"

"Sick bastard. Guess you're right. Look, your army's here now. We're gone. Good luck with this bastard. Hope you get him soon."

Mike watched Trace eyeball Sergio and suddenly Trace's face broke into a grin. "Tell her I'm on my way."

A look came over Sergio's face, shyness, sadness, a kind of self-deprecating look before he nodded. "Will do. Don't fuck around here too long, dude. She needs you tonight."

One minute the man was there and in seconds he'd faded into the night, his boys with him. Just before they were surrounded by squad cars, the SWAT vehicle and more cops than a military operation, Trace swore. "Fuck it, I'm going in." He checked his gun, found his flashlight, patted his vest looking for the extra clip and gave orders into his mic before creeping toward the door on the dark side of the building. Mike, his shadow, partner, friend fell in behind him.

The darkness hit them first. Outside, the moon had brightened the balmy air, giving them enough light to see. Inside, the tomblike darkness closed around them. Here the moon had no influence. It was dark, dank and disgusting.

Mike made sure they left the door slightly open in case they'd need backup and followed Trace to the stairs that must have led to other rooms above. He signaled they needed to clear this floor first and headed to his right while Trace took the left. Having worked together before, they knew instinctively what to expect from each other. They separated to scan the rooms.

Speaking quietly through their mic's, they all-cleared the first floor and met back at the stairs. They could hear sirens shutting down and the voices of the officers setting up for a long night. Shit! Mike could feel the tension build in his partner and knew that as the Chief of Police, McGuire could have stepped back, taken up the reins of command and simply gave orders. He also knew he hated asking another to do what he wouldn't do himself.

Guns aloft, listening to the silence and feeling his adrenaline going apeshit, he took the breath needed to stiffen his resolve and crept up behind Trace.

At the top of the stairs, the darkness was relieved by the few dirty and broken windows. It helped him make out the shapes of broken furniture and garbage strewn everywhere. Up here, the stench worsened, as if the mold and rotten food fought with the urine, making one choke on the mix. Littered with garbage and plastic bags, the disgusting floor looked worse than a dirty, dusty road. At least the weather cleaned that periodically whereas this filth here hadn't been scoured in years.

They hovered at the top of the stairs, waiting to see if they were going to draw any fire. So far, they still hadn't seen hide nor hair of the culprit. Feeling distinctively nervous, having no clue what to expect, but not willing to leave Trace's side, Mike stepped next to his boss and swept his flashlight over the small room.

Suddenly, from the other side of the building,

they heard gunfire. Mike knew their men were the targets and the prick they searched for wanted to take down as many as he could before he'd use his final bullet. *Sick bastard!*

Trace swatted his arm and pointed to the hall that would lead them to the killer. He nodded and headed in that direction, his flashlight shining directly to the floor to make sure he didn't trip on anything in his path or make unnecessary noise to warn their shooter he had company. Trace walked along beside him, both being super careful so they didn't alert the offender.

In unison they stopped, waiting until they heard his shooting start up again which would tell them he was too busy and wouldn't be aware that he'd been discovered. Tiptoeing forward, they both peered into the large, empty room that sheltered their man and slipped into the area... separating instinctively.

Mike finally saw the perp holed up at the largest window, a rifle in his hands and another near him on the floor. Dressed in camouflage, his face painted like a warrior, the young dude cackled with glee as he shot more rounds toward the crowd below.

From this angle, he'd say the man might be twenty but more likely younger. Doped up on nasty stuff that had likely destroyed whatever thought processes he had left, his frenzied chatter set Mike's radar on high. A guy like this was more dangerous than dynamite. He'd been taken over by shit that left him heartless, brainless and worst of all, fearless. He listened to the sick words coming from the assassin.

"Kill them. Kill everyone!" Bullets flew from his weapon. "Shoot the fuckers! Eh, eh! Got 'im. Yesss!"

With those words seared into his brain, Mike stepped out, took aim and fired at the same time as he yelled LVPD.

Trace's furious voice blended with his and his bullet hit the same target. "Shoot my men you bastard, and you're going down."

Chapter Ten

Leni stayed on autopilot, best sister in the world mode, and took all the shit Cass threw her way – the grumpy orders, the sarcastic comebacks from well-meaning requests. She didn't even flinch when she'd brought a requested warm blanket and had it chucked back at her in disgust.

"It's fucking hot in here, lady. Are you crazy?"

"You asked for a blanket. I got you a blanket. Hello?"

"I didn't ask for you to scald me with the fucker. Oh, God, this hurts." Cass grabbed at Leni's already sore hand, her nails clawing tiny pricks in the skin until blood appeared. "Shoot Trace for me. Promise. He gets to walk around, while I'm here in agony. All because he couldn't keep his hands to himself, the prick, asshole. Shoot the son of a bitch."

"You got it. I'll get right on that as soon as the baby's born."

"Baby? Right, I'm having a baby." Tears falling,

her face clearing, the madness receding, Cass reached for Faith who backed away in terror until she saw Cass's expression. "Faith, we're having a baby. I love babies. I love your Raoul. He's the most precious little guy in the world."

Faith, unable to refuse Cassi anything, stepped forward and leaned over. She used a cool cloth on Cass's forehead and spoke softly. "Your baby will be as beautiful. I have no doubt you and Trace have made a beautiful baby."

Eyes clouding over again, Leni saw the eruption and decided Faith was on her own. She stepped back just in time. Cassi, not able to grab for Leni, made a lunge at Faith. "This is all Trace's fault. Oh my God, the pain." Bent over, unable to speak, she clung to Faith's hand while Leni took a few moments to shake hers to get the blood flowing.

Jesus! She'd never have a baby if she had to go through this torture to give birth. Rethinking her decision to get married, knowing Mike wanted kids, she shuddered. That's when she noticed more blood had seeped from between Cass's legs, and she was panting before she suddenly grunted and began to push down.

The nurse, who'd stayed in the background most of the time, stepped forward to examine her patient and smiled gently. She patted Cassi's hand, whipping hers away before Cass could grab hold and spoke soothingly, "It'll be soon, Cassi. I can see the head crowning."

"She's crowning? Thank God." Trace filled the room with nervous energy and unfortunately bent over his wife.

Leni flinched and stepped even further into the background. Unable to help her *oh-oh* shit grin, she watched as Cass hauled off and punched the sucker. If Trace hadn't of had such quick reflexes to duck from the worst of the blow, he'd have ended up with his ass planted on the floor. As it was, he appeared shaken and wholly confused.

Before he could retaliate, or ask for explanations, Cass gave one last push, her screaming groan audible to anyone within a mile's vicinity, and Trace Junior, making a spectacular entrance, appeared in person.

Chapter Eleven

Sergio had taken up residence in the hallway. Leni spotted him there when she came looking for her fiancé. She watched as Mike approached him, shook his hand and spoke for a few minutes. The nurse who'd just left Cassi's room gave Sergio a thumbs up and whispered a message that made Sergio's face break from its normal brooding mask into a relieved grin. He noticed Leni, saw her expression and his became questioning. Then he shook his head as if to say not now and like ghosts, he and his bodyguard disappeared.

When Mike approached, Leni burst out, "What's that maniac doing here?" Disgusted, overwhelmed, yet sickened from the flooding hate, Leni saw Mike's eyebrow raise and an inquisitive look appear. "What's wrong, Leni? He's Cass's friend. Came to enquire about how she's doing. You know he watches over her – has since Raoul died."

"He should be in a cell, rotting like the rest of the animals who kill and don't care who gets hurt." Seeing Mike's expression change from worry to anger, she backed off and changed the subject. "Cass had her baby. It's a boy."

Mike whipped her into his arms and spun up the hallway, dancing like a foolish circus bear. "Trace is a daddy. A son! That's fantastic!"

"Put me down, you big lug." Leni couldn't help but laugh at his antics. "I've just decided that if you really want us to have kids, we'll be visiting an adoption agency. No way in hell I'm going through what Cass just did."

Mike grinned. "Okay by me, kiddo. How do you feel? You took a few good hits in the ring earlier, though it looked like you felt nothing. I've never seen you so focused, baby. You won that match like the pro you are."

"God, the fight seems like a lifetime ago. What time is it now?"

"Just a little after two a.m."

"Seriously? It seems like we've been in that hospital room for hours and hours."

"Actually, it's only been a little more than four hours since the fight. Cass has been very lucky. My sister was in labor for twenty-eight hours. Trust me, I heard all about it in glorious detail at the last family dinner. I told Mom there should be a law against us men having to listen to women's talk at the table, especially about having babies. And you know what she said?"

Leni, having fallen in love with Mike's mom and two sisters the first time she met them, laughed. "What did she say?"

"That if we got to enjoy the fun of making babies, we could damn well listen to the birth stories and be glad we weren't the ones with our legs straddling the delivery table."

Laughing at Mike's disgruntled expression, seeing the twinkle in his eyes he didn't try to hide, she responded, "Your mom was dead on. I totally agree."

"Shit, I kinda thought you would. Okay, let's go and meet the new McGuire Prince."

***

Leni stood back and watched as Mike approached Trace who was holding the little guy as if he held a precious, irreplaceable antique. Which, in fact, he did.

She saw the soft tenderness, the globby-eyed gaze, and the gentle way her bald-headed, green-eyed lover approached the infant. Emotions open for all to see, he smoothed his big hand tenderly over the tiny head and whispered loudly, "Hey, big guy. I'm your Uncle Mike and whoa, do I have stories to tell you about your old man."

Cassi, sitting up in bed, her earlier wild hair, smoothed and gathered into a ponytail, her face miraculously cleared, no longer mottled and glistening with sweat, laughed. "Hey, Mike! I need to hear those stories, too."

Trace spoke with authority, "Everything you talk about gets passed by me first."

Cassi winked at Mike. "Of course, it does dear heart. Of course."

Laughter filled the room. Knowing it was time to say good-night, Leni saw Faith sneaking out the door and quickly stopped her. "We'll drive you home, Faith. It's too late for you to be out alone."

"Great. I accept. Thanks. Steven was going to send a car from the casino, but I hate to bother him now. It might wake up Raoul, and you know what'll happen then." Faith blew kisses to Cass who returned them and waited for Leni and Mike to say their good-byes.

Trace, with his son held close, went over to Cassi and gingerly handed her their baby. Suddenly, he gathered both into his arms as if he had to be reassured that all was well. That's when Mike motioned for them to leave.

***

Mike knew what Trace had gone through earlier that same night, and though one flawed soul had returned to his maker and another appeared to spend this newest lifetime, Trace had been responsible for both happenings. And a man could only take so much.

Chapter Twelve

Weeks later, at home, after Cass had begun a routine living with a baby, a knock sounded at the door. She opened and her heart lifted. "Hi, Sergio. Come in. It's nice to see you."

Sergio, dressed like a normal guy rather than a gang boss with gold chains strung around his neck and more rings than a diva on his fingers, stepped inside and waved his bodyguard to hang out on the porch. "Is Bubba awake?" He pulled a huge brown, fuzzy teddy bear sporting a large blue satin bow out from behind his back.

Laughing, Cassi hugged Sergio first. Then she hugged the bear and slapped the beaming guy's arm playfully.

"Stop with the Bubba shit. His name is Nicolás. It's kind of a secret but that's Rusty's real name."

"Nico? I like it."

"Rusty was thrilled."

"No doubt. The baby couldn't have a better namesake. Rusty's a fighter, and I mean that literally and figuratively. Building up that kind of business, keeping it clean, took a lot of grit."

"With your help. The boys told me you shielded him from having to pay protection money to Dani way back. Now, having the US Featherweight champion as his fighter, the gym is being inundated with youngsters who want to train there, and they all want to work with him. The old devil's in his glory." Cassi reached for Sergio's hand and pulled him into the living room. "Can I get you a beer or a soft drink?"

"Sure. A coke is fine for me. Doug would probably crush on you even more if you took pity on him outside and gave him a cold beer. It's kind of warm out there."

"Okay. Wait here. I'll be back in a sec."

Cassi checked on the baby, hoping he might be awake so she could bring him out to Sergio for a visit and was thrilled when she saw him lying there quietly in the crib, kicking his legs and sucking on his tiny fist. Quickly changing his diaper and refitting him in his baby shorts and t-shirt outfit, she carried him out to the living room and laid him in the startled man's arms.

Dropping his phone by his side, Sergio took the baby gingerly, his face lit up with a grin not often seen. Then she fetched the drinks, making sure to drop off the beer to the bodyguard and share a few words first.

When she settled on the rug next to where Sergio was rocking a happy baby, she took a sip of her water. "Is this just a friendly visit or is there something on your mind?"

"Chick, you know me too well. I wanted to see this bambino, but I also wanted to ask you about Leni. She's shooting me daggers lately, and I need to know what's up."

"You noticed a change too. We're all in a quandary wondering what set her off. One day she was normal, happy... everything seemed okay. And suddenly, she switched... got attitude."

"Changed? How?"

"She's reverted back to the person I first met at Rusty's almost a year ago. We knew her as Arlene in those days. Back then, she had a disposition meaner than a maimed grizzly bear. But man could she handle herself in the ring. It's why Rusty stuck with her. He always saw her potential. We didn't know then she was a born fighter because of our father. Nor did we know she's my half-sister."

Sergio held Nico against his shoulder, all the while patting his back. "It's kind of weird the way Leni suddenly appeared at the gym, no? One minute she was in with the *Armas Jóvenes*, and the next, she'd pulled a disappearing act for months before showing up at Rusty's, working out and kicking ass."

"How did you know that?"

"When the news came out that she was your sister, I asked around. Seems her old lady pulled a disappearing act after she gave up the kid to her brother."

"I know. Leni accidentally learned about her mom by reading her diary. That's how we found out she was having an affair with José, mi papa. It says in the diary that they were going to run away together, or that's what Joan, Leni's mother, believed. She was only eighteen and in love with a man who had no business messing around with such a young girl. In the diary, she tells of how he turned mean after he lost the title match, changed into the jerk he could be when life didn't follow his plans. She wanted to get away from him, so she gave the baby to her brother, left and never returned. No one has any idea what happened to her."

"She never contacted them again?"

"Uh uh. Not that Leni knows, and she was really close to her Uncle Phil, Joan's brother. He would have confessed if he'd gotten any word from the woman. Leni told me he was dreadfully hurt and disappointed. He'd always believed something had happened to her to keep her away. After a few years, he filed a missing person's report, but it just gathered cobwebs in some busy cop's filing cabinet. Over time, I guess he lost hope and gave up."

"Do you think Leni'd like to meet up with the woman now? That's if she's still alive."

Cassi's antennae began to receive signals, and she perused his closed expression. "What're you saying?"

"I'm saying I know a guy."

"And...?"

"And, he finds missing people. You want I should contact him?"

"Jesus, Sergio. That's not a question for me to answer. But I'll ask Leni if you want and get back to you."

Sergio lifted the now fussing child and planted a big kiss on his forehead before passing him over to his mom. He stood and Cassi felt his hand caress her hair as he passed her on his way to the door. "You do that," he said, before it closed behind him.

Chapter Thirteen

For weeks, Leni's stomach gave her trouble, she was nervous and unable to sleep; her rioting emotions were driving her crazy. From the way people tip-toed around her, she supposed they had picked up on her crankiness and had no idea why she'd reverted back to being the girl whose life had always seemed bleak. The only respite from feeling trapped in the dark place was when she worked out, pounding on the punching bag or one of her sparring partners.

Surprised when Cassi called and invited her to the house, her tone not one that would easily accept a refusal, she decided to just get it over with. Mike had been on her case for days about her inactions with her sister and the baby. She needed to bring Nico a gift and officially welcome him to the family

Because of her mood, she'd put it off, making

excuse after excuse, her favorite that she wanted to give Cassi time to get settled. All bullshit of course. She couldn't bear bringing her hate-filled heart near that gorgeous little guy who she'd fallen in love with the moment he'd appeared. Both she and Mike had been completely smitten at the hospital and her views about adoption had disintegrated completely. Dreams of giving birth to her own baby replaced them.

Then there was Mike. He'd been on her case for days now and didn't understand that when her heart was so filled with hate, it hurt to be around happiness. It hurt when Cass showed her the loving kindness she'd lately taken to sharing. Hello hugs and loving glances had delighted her before the news had arrived that meant one of Cassi's special people was about to die, and Leni would be responsible.

Leni never did understand why Cass had such a tight relationship with Sergio Mandalas. Most knowing people in town feared him or bowed to him. He was the Top Gun in the distressed downtown district that thrived in the city of sin.

Even spending the smallest amount of time with Faith that she could get away with, she hated to see her friend's hurt when Leni couldn't be herself. Relaxing seemed impossible and enjoying the company of the woman who she so admired and loved dearly was a huge stress rather than the fun it used to be. Right from the beginning, after Faith had saved her from being raped by a fat slug that meant to take his pleasure and wouldn't take no for an answer, Leni had let Faith in, became her friend, and they'd gotten closer as time went on. Now, she pretended not to see text messages and didn't answer when the caller showed as Faith.

And Mike, he was ready to tear his hair out, or more likely, hers. He'd shown more patience than a high-paid shrink, and she knew it wasn't easy for him. He'd tried in many ways to get her to open up, share her nightmare... let him in.

She just couldn't. Really, how would it sound if she told her cop boyfriend that she wanted to kill the man responsible for Mani's death?

Shit – shit, shit, shit!

She couldn't see straight anymore, and tears hovered all the time. Torn, terribly unhappy, unsure of the future and scared of her own thoughts, she pulled up outside of Cass's place and sat with her head on the steering wheel. *Oh, God. Take this madness out of my heart. Help me shake off this horrible nightmare.*

Lifting the tiny pair of boxing gloves she'd had made and hauling the giftwrapped fancy new stroller from the back of the car, she slowly approached the house, overcoming her panic. Fighting off the urge to drop everything and run, she lifted the heavy parcel higher and stepped over the curb.

Before she reached the sidewalk to Cass's old

house a woman approached and stopped her. Whether it was her bearing – that of a person screaming money, or the look on her high-classed, well-groomed face, her dark hair shiny and obviously styled by a professional – Leni didn't know. Maybe it was the instant bond between them, the knowing here was the missing parent she'd never met, Leni didn't care. All she knew was her mother stood there in front of her, and she dropped her parcels, fisted her hands and prepared for the battle of her life.

Chapter
Fourteen

"Arlene? Arlene Montgomery?"

"Not anymore. My name is Leni Santino now."

"I see. You changed your name for the last fight. You used to fight under Arlene Montgomery."

"Yeah, well, I've had a few different names. What do you want?"

"Do you know who I am?"

"Yeah. You're Joan Montgomery, my old lady." Being rude and abrupt on purpose, Leni watched the woman flinch, but not back down.

"Like you, I also changed my name. I'm now, Deputy Director of the Central Intelligence Agency, Lorraine Sedol."

"Holy shit! Seriously?" Stunned, Leni's purposely cavalier attitude changed to shock and awe.

"Yes. It's one of the reasons I've stayed away from you for so long. My position holds a certain amount of responsibility, but unfortunately, it also brings restrictions and often danger to those close to me."

"You're saying you stayed away from us all this time for *our* safety. Lady, give me a break. I don't believe you. Over the years, Uncle Phil yearned to see you. He searched until there was no place left to look and no one really interested in helping him."

"I'm so sorry about his passing. I hoped to be able to see him before he died. To thank him for looking after you. I always meant to return for you."

"Yet you didn't."

Lorraine bowed her head. "No, I didn't. Instead, I worked three jobs to get through law school, telling myself you needed a mother who could support you. Then, I was offered an internship with—"

Interrupting excuses she didn't want to hear, Leni yelled, "I don't give a fuck about what stopped you from being my mom. I just know in the big scheme of things, I didn't matter enough." Lowering her voice when she felt Cassi step in behind her, sheltering her, she added, "Why have you come now?"

Lorraine eyed the other girl, but she stayed focused on Leni. "I had to. I've been watching over you, but there was some time when you were lost to me. I had no idea what had happened until I saw the fight against Charo Hall and recognized you. You're like your father in the ring. Beautiful to watch and brutally powerful."

Cassi interrupted. "Would you ladies like to bring this inside? The neighbors are getting an eyeful. They've never seen a motorcade on this street before."

"Yes. I would like that. I need to talk to you, Arl... Leni, if it's okay with you."

"Yeah, well it isn't. Okay with me." Leni, knowing her look could scald, turned to Cassi. "Sorry, sis. I can't do this." Passing over the smaller parcel and motioning to the larger giftwrapped box holding the stroller, she added, "Give the little man a hug for me. Tell him I'll be back. Here're his presents from me and his Uncle Mike."

Walking backwards while talking, she got into the driver's side of her car, turned on the ignition and threw it into drive – all in one action – then squealed away from the curb. In the rear view, she saw two startled women, one holding a gift. The other in tears.

Chapter Fifteen

Cass didn't know what to say. She saw the tears the other woman shed, and something shifted inside her heart.

The older woman rubbed at her eyes with trembling fingers and spoke in a low tone, "May I take you up on your kind offer to come inside for a few minutes?"

Soft-hearted, Cassi fought with her conscience and gave in to her curiosity. She hoped Leni wouldn't be pissed at her for allowing Joan access, but something had happened to Leni to turn her into the old version, and Cass would do anything to get her back. If her mother was the reason, Cass wanted to know.

"You didn't hear the part where I introduced myself. My name is now Lorraine Sedol—"

"You're the Deputy Director for the Central Intelligence Agency."

Obviously shocked that she was recognized, Lorraine nodded, her bearing suddenly looking frail, even sickly, and Cassi became concerned. "Of course, please come into the house and get out of the sun. Vegas afternoons can be brutal at this time of the year."

"I do understand. Virginia can be as bad. But I've had a tiring trip and would appreciate a cold glass of water and to be able to sit."

Cassi changed Leni's gift to her left hand and using her right, she reached for the other's arm and helped her up the stairs and into the house. Glad that Nico was sleeping, she settled her guest in the living room and fetched the box from the front yard before getting the pitcher of iced tea and platter of biscuits she'd prepared for her and Leni to share.

Settled next to the woman who now sat back in the chair, her right foot up on the leg rest, Cassi waited for the other to begin the conversation.

"I don't usually collapse in front of people. I'm quite strong normally, but I've had a knee replacement a few weeks ago, and it's taking it's time to heal."

"No doubt it's still painful. Doesn't it take months for the swelling to go down and the pain to disappear?"

"Thank goodness, no. My doctor assured me it would be much less painful in a few more weeks, as long as I elevate it periodically and keep up my exercises."

"So, you're on a medical leave and had some time on your hands. Decided to look up your daughter and say hello?" Cass knew they needed to talk about what mattered and how long they'd have before Nico got hungry and demanded his mom's attention was anyone's guess. "I'm sorry to be so blunt, but I don't understand. Were you surprised when Leni called me sis? We are, you know. Sisters that is. Well, half-sisters. My father was also José Santino."

Ashamed and wearing her remorse for Cass to see, Lorraine nodded. "As I said to Ar-Leni, I've followed her career, and it was all over the news when you fought Ariana Wilde. Then it came out soon after that you were José's daughter and that Leni was your half-sister."

Cass could see that the woman was working out what to say next, and the words she finally released, shocked Cassi and had her full attention.

"I'm being blackmailed."

"Excuse me? Blackmailed? You mean about Leni being your daughter?"

"Yes, something like that. You see, I've been invited to run for Senator and decided I would. Except for my earlier life, I've lived very quietly. I've never married, have no other children and basically remained faithful to my job. For years, I was a CIA operative and seldom in the US, so I never settled into the typical woman's role."

"Is that why you ignored your child?"

Stunned, chastened but accepting the truth of the statement, Lorraine admitted, "Mostly. Once the first years passed while I struggled through college, and I was in a position where I could afford to give her a home, I was never in it. I spent more time abroad involved in political affairs in other countries, often in danger and usually gone for months on end. How could I give Leni the kind of home a child needs? Plus, at Phil's she had Mani, her cousin. And she loved him. I saw her with him in their yard, playing basketball. They looked so happy. By then, I couldn't take her away from the only home she knew."

Cassi listened, and it dawned on her that the woman had obviously been truthful about watching over Leni. She just hadn't realized that it meant she'd physically been around. Spying, stalking... eavesdropping. A terrible sadness appeared and struck her hard. Trying to fit herself in that position, a mother who loved her child so much that she did what she thought was best for the girl.

If the roles were reversed, could she stay away from Nico? Never in a million years... unless. Lordy... unless it was for his own good. Could she? *Jesus!*

Lorraine finally looked up and saw the frown Cassi didn't hide. "When she got older and into trouble, running wild with that crazy Juan Acedo, I did step forward. I was scared. I couldn't find Leni, so I contacted Mani."

"What? You approached Mani?"

"Yes. That was before he joined the gang. He'd just found out what had happened to Arlene, as she was called in those days, and he had plans."

"He joined the gang himself."

"Yes. My nephew was a very smart young man, very talented. Did you know he wanted to be an artist? And he was brilliant. Anyway, he'd run into her and came up with the idea that if he could insinuate himself into a top position, he could orchestrate a kind of release for her. He contacted me and let me in on his plans. He saw how unhappy she was and wanted her to be free to move on and make something of her life. He only planned to stick with the gang for a short time. He wanted to work out a plan with the other local gang leader to take over, then he'd be free to walk away. He knew Sergio Mandalas, had met with him, and they'd discussed the possibility of this happening. Part of the results would be freedom for Mani. But after he got killed, of course, that didn't transpire. Thankfully, Leni was still free to move on."

Shocked, yet accepting the truth of what Lorraine said, Cassi added, "What I understand from the little Leni's talked about her past, she couldn't leave Vegas because her Uncle Phil was terminal with cancer, and she loved him too much to disappear. She'd stayed in hiding and only showed up at the end. It was a terrible time for her. In those days, she didn't get on with her Aunt Barb, her beloved uncle was dying, and Mani was gone. She could have used a mom."

"No doubt. But not one she hated. I thought to step forward. I did go to Mani's funeral, but no one recognized me. I saw her with my brother, and I had to accept that it was his time to have her with him. I'd given up the right."

Heartbreak showed on the features of a woman filled with remorse. And Cassi felt the waves of sadness radiating around her. She didn't know what to say except for the one phrase a person could use in these circumstances. She reached for Lorraine's hand and spoke gently. "I'm so sorry. Life's been a bitch for you. You made choices and lived with them. I respect that. But what a terrible price you've paid."

Lorraine squeezed Cassi's fingers, fumbled to stand and dropped back as if she hadn't the stamina. "I'd given up hope that I could ever reach out to my daughter, but this nightmare has forced my hand. I won't be blackmailed. I'll refuse to pay the ten million dollars they asked to keep this breaking news from coming out. But I couldn't let them do so until I had personally contacted Leni to warn her about what was going to happen. She'll be inundated with news people and the paparazzi, all wanting her story."

"Fuck! That'll drive her insane. And she's already unsteady lately. None of us understand why she's carrying this particular monkey on her back, or even what it's about; she won't share with her friends, even her fiancé. We're all worried, that's why I insisted she come see me today. Now this? It'll be too much."

Shooting forward in her chair, a shrewd expression settling on her still-lovely face, Lorraine demanded answers. "What's happened? You say she changed? Has she already been approached? She knew me instantly. I didn't expect that." Lorraine pounded her fist on the armrest and growled, "I'll blasted well pay the money if it stops Leni from doing something stupid. I know she's volatile, like her father. My poor girl."

"Do you know who it is that's blackmailing you?"

"Not really. I've sorted out the most logical, of course being my opponents for the Senator's seat, but I can't imagine any of them stooping so low."

"It's politics, Lorraine."

"Yes, that's true. It could be a person who just wants to pay me back for past incidents. Who knows? I've certainly been involved in a lot of traumatic episodes with let's say nefarious people, so I do have enemies. I've asked for time and they gave me until midnight. By then if I haven't followed their arrangements for payment, they'll break the story."

"So, we have to get Leni here so you two can talk, and she'll know what to say to the reporters. Is that what you want?"

"God, no. I don't want her to feel in any way indebted to me. She certainly has no reason to be. I just wanted her to be prepared. She's free to tell the reporters whatever she wants. My answer will be "no comment." I've prepared a written statement to be released after the news comes out and it's very brief and to the point."

"About Leni?"

"Yes. It will simply say that I did have a child when I was eighteen and that my brother's family raised her while I continued to serve my country within the Central Intelligence Agency. We're not close, but I love her dearly and wish her all the happiness in the world."

"Doesn't Leni have the right to hear you say those words to her first? Even if she rejects them and wants nothing to do with you?"

"Absolutely. It's why I'm here."

Chapter Sixteen

Leni couldn't believe that her mother, a woman she'd never met, would be so brazen as to approach her on a sidewalk in front of Cassi's home and want to talk. *Talk!* Goddamn, that takes more than guts. It shows a kind of disrespect to Leni, a downplaying of her rights. As if being a CIA agent takes precedence. The fucking audacity of the bitch to expect instant obedience... and a hearing, when she's been absent all Leni's life.

Leni drove for hours and had no idea where she went. Knowing her attention wasn't on the road after she almost hit a cyclist, she pulled over, and sat in the parked car. With her head leaning against the headrest, she scrubbed at her eyes for the hundredth time and decided... *yet again...* she shouldn't shed one fucking tear for the woman whose hungry gaze had ripped her to shreds. Those sorrow-filled eyes became hooded once Leni spoke, but not quick enough that Leni missed the eager, loving, joy the woman took too long to hide.

Angrier than she could remember ever feeling before, Leni cussed a blue streak and ended up screaming her rage to the sounds of the music playing on her radio. A man walking past the car looked in, frowned and quickened his step.

You're scaring people you idiot. Stop the hysteria and while you're at it, stop with the theatrics too. You're overreacting and you know it. So you're long lost mother approached you. Big hairy shit. So she's not dead or lost her memory or any one of the hundred excuses you've given her over the years to explain why she left you. Just face it, the lady moved on. Left you with people she knew would look after you... love you. And she didn't give a shit. So what. You aren't the only person in the world not wanted by their mother. Suck it up.

She blew her nose, used the comb from her purse, then headed for the nearest bar which happened to be the Lipstick Club, Cassi's old stomping grounds and the place where Mani was killed.

Chapter Seventeen

"Cassi, have you seen Leni? I got home from work late, and she wasn't here, I can't reach her on her cell, nor has she answered my texts."

"Hi, Mike. I'm so glad you called. I tried to get through to you earlier, but they said you were busy and couldn't be reached. I left messages."

"Yeah, I saw them. It's why I called. What's up?"

"About Leni, I didn't know if she would share it with you or not, but there was a bit of a situation at the house earlier today."

"A situation? She said she was going over to see Nico and bring the baby his gift. She was excited to see your face when you saw the boxing gloves she had made for Nico."

"She did drop off the gifts, but she didn't stay, Mike. Her mother was here—"

"Her mother! Did I hear that right?"

"Yeah, crazy, right? The woman approached her

out of the blue, and Leni kind of lost it. Said a few things she needed to get off her chest and took off like a bat out of hell. Her mother is Lorraine Sedol, Deputy Director of the Central Intelligence Agency."

Mike whistled. "Her long lost mother! Seriously? She's Lorraine Sedol?" He whistled again. "I've met the woman. She's a hard-ass, a person most people step around rather than approach, unless your position is high enough that no one scares you." Mike's chuckle had no humor at all. "So that's Leni's mother? Christ, that also means she'll be my mother-in-law. Oh man, a guy just can't catch a break. First, she turns all moody and weird so I can't get near her and now this. Do you think this is why she's been acting so strange lately?"

"I don't think so. Leni looked completely shocked when Lorraine approached. I'd been on the porch waiting for her to show up and saw it all."

"So, Leni wouldn't talk to her."

"Nope. But Lorraine was recuperating from a knee replacement and needed to sit down. She came inside for a while after Leni left, and as far as she knew, Leni had no knowledge of her or her position."

"So why now? What drove her out of the bushes? Atonement? What? Now that Leni's famous, she wants a place in her life?"

"Nothing like that, Mike. She came to warn Leni. The woman's going to be running for

Senator, and she's being blackmailed about giving up her baby. She doesn't intend to pay, so it's bound to come out. Warning Leni first was something she needed to do. As it turns out, if the woman is to be believed, and I did, she's been following Leni's life all along, just never approached, never wanted to interfere in what looked to her to be the perfect world that Leni lived in. If you can find her and bring her back here, I'll explain it all."

"Where do you think she'd go?"

"I called the gym and Rusty hasn't seen her, neither has Faith. Her Aunt Barb is away in Florida right now so she's not there. I don't know where else to call."

"Right, I'll put out an APB on her license plates and see if we get a hit. I'll get back to you."

"Okay, and Mike... she was really upset. I'm worried."

"Me too, Cass. That girl's an active volcano ready to blow."

Chapter Eighteen

Leni sat at the dimly lit Lipstick Club, the place where Cass used to work, and tried to ignore the stench of weed and alcohol that permeated the place. Sitting at the bar, she gulped back her third vodka shooter then chased it with her third beer. When another text message showed up, she checked her phone. Rather than answer, she closed it and shrugged. Man those friends of hers were ganging up. She'd had a number of messages from Cassi, then Faith and of course, Mike. But having nothing to say to any of them made replying too difficult to cope with, and so she just ignored them all.

Glancing around and seeing so many losers ranging from underage to old wannabes with white hair and beards, they sat, shooting the shit and drank to get drunk. The servers mostly talked amongst themselves and ignored the customers, until they got rowdy in their demands.

When one of the men approached, she didn't even look up, just told the guy to fuck off and ignored his reaction. Her attitude wasn't friendly or welcoming, exactly the way she felt. That was until she heard a voice she recognized. Doug. He was at Cassi's wedding with Sergio. In fact, he was often with Sergio, probably worked as his bodyguard. An idea struck. If she could get this guy to take her to Sergio, she could exact her revenge. Make him pay for what he did to Mani. Then maybe she could sleep again.

Now wouldn't that piss off her big-shot mom, a jailbird for a daughter, charged with murder and pleading guilty?

Doug ordered a beer and took the chair two down from hers, leaving the one in between empty. Leni glanced up and sure enough, it was the same guy she remembered.

"Hey, you're Doug, right? You were at Cassi Santino's wedding."

Doug glanced over, his expression empty, not welcoming, nor denying her claim. At first, he didn't answer until he'd taken a closer look. Then his expression changed, a grin lit up his face. "You're Cass's sister, the fighter."

"Yeah, I'm Leni Santino." She moved to the empty seat between them, held out her hand and was shocked at the welcome now showing on Doug's face. He grasped her hand in the typical shake amongst the gang members. "You come here all the time?" She wanted to keep him talking and try to get information.

"Nah, it reminds me too much of the past. But Sergio likes to keep an eye on things in the area, likes to know if anything is brewing, and there's always a lot of bullshit thrown around about this time of night. By now, the boys are usually half cut and yappy."

Leni added, "Sergio Mandalas, he took over the *Armas Jóvenes* gang after Dani Andino and Billy died, right?"

"That's right. But what a lot of people don't know is that *Los Soldados* were here first. The others barged in and wanted it all to themselves. Now, we're back to the way it should be. There's peace on the streets again. No more fighting and revenge shootings."

Surprise – that's what you think! Leni didn't speak her thoughts, but they were in her head. Not paying any attention to what was happening in the rest of the club, she tried to keep Doug involved in their discussion. "Does Sergio come here too? Or he probably has his own hangout bar, right?"

"Nah, he don't like these kinds of places. He mostly hangs at Sam's Pub where they have pool tables. He's hot for the game, likes to play."

She stored that information and kept Doug talking. "Did you know the guy who called himself Mani Abel?"

Doug swiveled to confront her. "I did. He was a good guy. Dani had him working with her, second-in-command. I liked him. The man knew how to get loyalty and work with the guys. Most of the boys would've laid down their lives for him."

Surprised at the tone of respect and the kind words, Leni admitted, "He was my cousin. We grew up together." The next words out of her mouth never happened. She was cut off by the voice of her fiancé.

"Hey, darlin' you havin' fun?"

Leni had been so involved in her discussion with Doug, she hadn't seen Mike arrive. He leaned against the counter, on the other side of her, near the seat where she'd sat earlier. He motioned to the bartender to give him a beer. "Hey, Doug. How's things?"

"Good, Officer Kowalski. How're you?" Doug used Mike's title on purpose, and it got a smile from Mike.

"Sweet and sassy. Looking for crooks to arrest so my numbers stay up."

Doug laughed, knowing by Mike's wink and tone, he was messing around. "Good to see you. You too, Leni. Take care y'all."

Leni watched as Doug strode over to a table full of drunken idiots and took a seat.

Shit! Shit, shit, shit!

"I've been looking all over for you." Mike's tone changed from joking to serious. "What's up,

Leni?"

Knowing she wouldn't get anywhere with Mike hovering around, she decided to give up her mission for tonight and maybe find a way to contact Doug another time. At least she now had a lead. She knew where she'd likely be able to find her prey.

Chapter Nineteen

Mike couldn't believe his eyes when he entered the disgusting place and sure enough, there was his fiancée schmoozing with some guy from one of the local gangs. It was only after he got closer and saw who had her attention that he relaxed and let go of his anger. After all, Doug had been at Trace and Cassi's wedding and was considered a friend. Who was he to repudiate that and turn all suspicious?

Plus, Leni hadn't appeared nervous or worried for him to find her with the guy. Relieved, he decided to play it low-key and not accuse her of misbehaving. Though she had. Taking off without any explanations, going AWOL for hours, making him rely on the LVPD officers on duty to find her license plate and send him the info.

It sucked. He didn't like it, especially not for the woman he wanted desperately to make his wife and certainly not for the future mother of his kids.

Her behavior had been unacceptable lately, and his first reaction was to confront her in the open and lay everything on the table, then deal with the mess. That was his way. How his parents had brought him up. Nothing stays buried, that's if you want a healthy relationship.

Unfortunately, her response to trauma was to wall everything up inside, sneak around and go it alone.

"You ready to leave?"

***

She looked at him and could tell he'd pretty much reached the end of his rope. Oh, God! Losing him would kill her. She'd rather die than not have him in her life. She needed to fix this with him. And with Cassi and Faith. But that meant giving up her plans to get Sergio. So, maybe she didn't need to actually kill the loser. What if she just got him to admit to shooting her Mani, and they put him away for the rest of his life. Now that she could deal with.

"I'm sorry, Mike. Please – just take me home."

He stared into her eyes and must have seen the gleam she didn't try to hide, the flame that used to be there all the time. The one that said she loved him; needed him. She prayed he wouldn't destroy the moment by being all cop-like and confrontational. "Okay, baby. Let's take my car and pick yours up in the morning. We'll go home and make up."

Moving in close, feeling his arm around her body, being hugged to his side, she laid her head on his shoulder, reached to kiss his neck and let him lead her to his car. They stopped in the dark of the parking lot, and he kissed her until her head spun. His lips had a way of drawing everything she had right out from her very soul. No one else could ever stir her the way he could. Trembling, breathing hard, she pushed her body closer, encouraging him. If he'd have wanted to take her there and then, spread her over the hood of his car and have his way with her, she'd have let him. The magic surrounding them was so powerful, she couldn't have refused.

Instead, he hugged her hard one last time and then shuffled her into the passenger seat, groaning his frustration. Then he settled behind the wheel and after one last deep kiss, he wheeled out of the lot. "You sure know where the hell to pick your spots to turn all sexy and flirty, baby. Wait till I get you home, you'll pay for that tease."

Laughing, her voice husky with desire, she lifted his hand from the steering wheel and held it against her breast, rubbing it back and forth, provocative, cheeky... loving the power when he groaned again.

"Stop it, witch. I have to drive. Instead of tormenting me, you need to call Cass."

Still fuzzy-headed and feeling hot for her man, she denied his request and said, "Don't want to.

Don't want to talk. Just want to make love."

"Sorry, honey. This is really important and for your own good. She has some news you need to hear."

"Not now. For Christ's sake. I'm serious Mike. I have nothing to say to her tonight. Besides it's too late."

"Trust me, she won't care."

"I'll call her in the morning." Sitting straight, most of the alcohol induced fog clearing, she made up her mind not to be bullied into doing something she didn't want to do. Thinking of Cass led her mind to her mother, and she definitely didn't want to go there. Not when she was feeling so good.

Hearing the determination in her voice, Mike knew that to push the issue was to lose her for that night, and it had been so long since he'd felt their connection. He'd go in late in the morning so he could hang with her while she made the call, protect her from the coming shock. But tonight, he wanted his girl hot and bothered with loving on her mind, not anger.

He reached across and caressed her cheek before taking her hand again and squeezing. "If that's your decision, baby, then I'll shut up and let you take lead. We'll deal with Cass and her news in the morning. Tonight will be for us."

Happy again, she cooed her acceptance and kissed his fingers. "Then let's get home."

"You got it." He turned on the siren to the sound of her giggling and got them home in a very few minutes. Then he playfully lifted her over his shoulder and carried her into the apartment.

Chapter Twenty

Once inside their suite, Mike closed the door, let her slide down his body until her feet were almost touching the floor. He held her there, so their eyes were on the same level, and he huskily whispered, "Hi, sweetheart."

Wrapping her legs around his waist, she answered, "Hi, handsome." Leni loved his strength and the way he made her feel so precious and tiny. She wasn't a big woman, but she was all muscle and often felt strong rather than feminine.

Mike's size and the gentle way he used it was perfect. Respect for her was always plain to see, plus his love and admiration. What more could a girl ask for in her man? She kissed his bald head teasingly, the way she liked to do to make him smile. Hands on both sides of his face, she peered into his eyes and saw the adoration he never hid, the complete trust he showed her and his profound need to be loved buried deep that called to her.

This man didn't give his love easily. He'd strung their romance out, wouldn't have sex with her until he felt they'd built a relationship first. Old-fashioned to a fault, he believed in all those quaint old philosophies about faithfulness, and honor, respect and decency. Finding this man had been the best thing that had ever happened to her and like a flash of clarity, she knew she could only push him so far. Once he'd had enough, he'd walk away and it would be her choice, her fault... her doing.

Fear rushed in, and she whispered, "Mike, I need you so much, love you so much. Don't ever leave me."

"The only way you could ever get rid of me, drive me away from you, was if you pushed me past what I could bear. And baby, I have a huge tolerance for those I love. We'll work everything out." His gaze adored her, and she felt instant relief.

As they headed into the bedroom, they kissed. While a sexy awareness permeated, surrounding them... closing them into a lover's circle... the rest of the world faded.

He stood her by the bed and began undressing her slowly, calling out to Alexa to play their favorite song. The low music added to the romance as he listened to her sing the words he loved to hear, her sweet voice winding through his heart and making the moment one he'd never forget.

Love filled the semi-dark room, and they were enfolded in it's magic.

Sensing that he wanted to be the one to disrobe her, she stood quietly singing, letting him have his way. He kissed every inch that became naked, and her soaring voice trembled with desire, but as if she were under a spell, she sang on. He'd begun working on his own clothes and by the end of the song, they both stood naked.

Swaying now, the music alive in her head, she reached to hug him close, knowing as soon as he felt her body slide against his, he'd lose control and nature would take over. And that's exactly what happened. Her breasts pushed into his chest, the hair tickling as it always did, but not distracting her from her purpose. When she mashed her groin against him, she felt his grow with excitement, and knew she'd be pleasured into screaming her release.

The thought had her breathing quicken and soon they were both panting with need.

That's about the time her legs weakened, and she pulled him with her as she fell back on the bed, thankful it was so close. Once he nestled on top of her, ecstasy vibrating between them, their kisses grew even more heated. Suddenly, his lips left hers to travel down her throat and to her breasts where his hands had been gently kneading, awakening the erogenous zones, forcing the mounds to swell, inflaming her nipples so a sweet ache began ripping through her body to the hot, wet, needy entrance yearning to be penetrated.

Aroused past bearing, shuddering, Leni's voice hoarse with need, she spoke, "Mike, now. Please. I need you inside me."

"Yes, baby. You're ready. You're so wet." Panting, writhing with passion, he took both her hands in his, lay them over her head and entered her with one plunge. He groaned his pleasure, their voices ringing together, and he began to move slowly.

Not willing to wait, reverberating with passion, aroused as never before, Leni pushed her body up to his, taking him in so deeply that he had no choice but to react. Straining, his hard thrusts gratifying, the stimulation soon became satisfaction that cascaded over her hot, sweaty body. Moans of appreciation escaped while she twitched and shuddered from their union.

He wasn't quite ready to end the pleasure and his last thrusts penetrated deeper, bringing more pleasure, her body rippling with pulsations, dizzy from the immense pleasure.

Mike let her hands go and scooped her close. Nestling her head on his shoulder, she gently filtered her fingers through the hair on his chest and accepted once and for all, she needed him in her life, or she might as well be dead.

As if he'd heard her thoughts, his voice whispered the words she'd been thinking, "I love you, Leni. I'd never want to live without you, so you gotta stay safe baby. Always be safe."

Chapter Twenty-one

As promised, Leni called Cassi in the morning before Mike left for work and agreed to be there as soon as she picked up her car.

Mike hugged her from behind and kissed her neck. "I'll drive you to the club first. Then I'll follow you to Cassi's."

"You don't have to come with me, Mike. I'll be fine alone."

"Not this time, honey. We do this together."

Stiffening and not able to stop herself, she spit out, "Look, if you know what she's going to tell me, why don't you save me the trip."

"Don't be pissy, girl. I don't know everything that happened, and Cassi does. Let's do this my way with no arguments, okay. Please."

"Fine." Leni grudgingly acquiesced, swallowing her fear of getting hurt by words she wasn't sure she was ready to hear.

***

They arrived at Cassi's together and holding hands, they entered the house to see Nico in the stroller that Leni had left at the house the day before, his tiny new boxing gloves tied across the bars so he could push and wave at them like babies tended to do with anything in their eyesight.

"Oh, Lordy, that's so cute. He likes his gloves." Leni crouched down next to the little guy and held her finger for him to grasp. Nico desperately tried to hold her gaze, but his head wobbled too much to allow him more than a few seconds.

Mike motioned to pick him up but first asked, "May I?"

Cassi grinned proudly. "Of course, Uncle Mike. He loves to be cuddled." But cuddling made the baby sleepy and within a few seconds, Mike sat quietly, holding him close while Leni watched adoringly.

Cassi grinned. "He does that to Trace all the time. As soon as he picks him up, Nico falls asleep and Trace hardly ever gets to see him in action. And trust me, he's growing like a weed, has a cry like a banshee and can coo forever when he has someone paying him attention."

Leni finally pulled her hungry gaze away from her nephew and looked at Cass to see her shrewd eyes watching, waiting. "Okay, out with it. What's up?"

"Have you seen the news on TV this morning?"

"Nope."

"It's probably best for me to show you and then explain." Cassi turned on the kitchen TV and Leni saw her mother on the screen in a news conference, the reporters flocked around, yelling questions and hounding the pale woman. Her comments were short, just a few words, but they drilled into Leni, making the pain raw and horrible. Mike laid the baby in the stroller and came to her at the same time as Cass had drawn her close.

"Lorraine came to warn you about this yesterday, it's why she showed up out of the blue. Someone was blackmailing her for ten million dollars to stop the story, and she refused to pay the money. She knew that even if she paid, the story would still come out, just maybe not this quick."

Leni's throat felt like she had to drive her words through a wall of cement, the shock hit so hard. "Sh-she came to warn me that soon the whole world would know I was unwanted. A baby she left without a care in the world, never looking back or regretting her decision. And I'm supposed to thank her for her thoughtfulness?"

"Lord, no, Leni. It's not that way at all. You don't understand. I'm not even sure I do, but she isn't the callous, hardhearted person you're trying to make her out to be. She didn't just throw you away and never look back. She followed your life, every aspect of your years growing up. The reason she didn't approach you was her misguided notion that fetching you to live in her world would bring you loneliness, insecurity, and even danger. As a CIA operative, she was never home, and she'd seen how happy you were with Phil and Mani. She couldn't bring herself to tear you away. Putting your welfare and best interests over her wants wasn't easy. I'm not even sure it was the right thing to do. That choice wouldn't have been mine... I think. But when it comes to what's best for your child, I guess a mother has to make some hard decisions. Before you condemn her, hear her out."

Leni listened to Cass, heard her words and for the first time, something besides anger and resentment reached her brain. Crazy but true, she wanted to believe her mother had cared for her. That she hadn't just left her without any qualms or regrets.

"Cass, you think I should meet with her? Mike?"

Both replied in the affirmative, Mike adding his thoughts, "Cass says she's thinking to run for Senator. But this might kibosh her plans."

"So that's why she's coming forward now, because the news might turn the people against her."

Cass, ever truthful, especially after living with a past full of lies, admitted, "Honey, I don't know. She seemed sincere in her love for you. She told me that her and Mani had worked together to get you—"

"Whoa, back up. She talked to Mani?" A load of

bricks had just dropped on her head. "Okay, I need to meet with the woman. The sooner the better. Can you arrange it?"

Chapter
Twenty-two

Mike decided to hang around for the upcoming meeting. No way he wanted his girl to be blindsided by more information than she could handle, especially in her already weak state of mind. He watched as Cass called the number from the card Lorraine had left behind. In a very few minutes, it was decided that Lorraine would come back to see Leni here as soon as her driver could get her here. At least she wasn't slotting her daughter into an appointment, making her wait.

They passed the short while in conversation about Nico and his baby habits, Cass, no doubt, trying to keep Leni's mind from traveling back to whatever had disrupted her world before.

They made a pot of coffee and Leni helped put out the biscuits and cut up some fruit. Before they'd finished setting the table up in the living room, Lorraine knocked at the door and hustled quickly into the room.

Wearing a man's large grey hoodie that hid most of her clothes and her face, looking like a street person, she hovered by the door uncomfortably. "My driver thinks we got away from the reporters, but they have ways of miraculously finding people. I didn't want to bring them here, so we used Kevin's personal car. He's my driver. Kevin that is. This is his sweater." Rambling, she removed it but clung to the garment as if it gave her strength.

Mike had met the woman before and had seen the respect she drew from everyone near her, the confidence she exuded and the hard-eyed gaze that never changed while she stayed in public. In contradiction, here was a woman, distraught, scared, wobbly and totally unlike the person he'd expected.

Cassi stepped forward to take the sweater and motioned Lorraine into the living room where they had set the table. "We made coffee and a little snack. Please come in and sit so we can talk."

Mike noticed that Leni hadn't moved. She just stared at her mother as if making up for years of not being able to. Catching her gaze, Lorraine didn't flinch. Her fearful expression didn't change. There was a glow deep in her eyes that Mike had seen many times in his mother's. He motioned to Cass and pushing Nico's stroller back into the kitchen, they left the other two alone.

Once they'd closed the kitchen door so they

couldn't be heard, Mike sighed long and loud. "I gotta admit I don't know how this will turn out. Leni has issues going on right now, and she won't divulge anything she's thinking. But I can see she's suffering."

"I know. I finally remembered that the day this all seemed to begin, she'd had lunch with Flossie, one of the barmaids that used to work at the Lipstick Club. I guess they knew each other from the past. I didn't have her number, but Trace got it for me, so I called her this morning. At first, she couldn't think of what might have triggered Leni, but she did say they'd talked about the night Mani died. She'd told Leni she'd always believed that Sergio Mandalas had pulled the trigger of the gun that had killed Mani."

"Shit."

"I know, right? Except, that's isn't true. I know for a fact, he didn't. I was there and saw the man whose hands were tattooed. Sergio's are too, but he's shorter than the guy who shot up the club, shorter and less heavy. I've been wondering if maybe she's gotten it into her head that she needs revenge for Mani's death. I certainly know how that feels. She loved him like a brother, they were very close."

Mike thought about Cassi's words, and they rang true. It certainly could be that gossip eating away at Leni all this time.

"What did her mother have to say about Mani?"

Maybe if he knew, he could get a better feel for the man and figure out what had happened in the past.

"Lorraine said she'd been following Leni's progress, even going as far as stalking her, watching them grow up from afar. She mentioned spying while they played basketball in their yard and how happy they'd looked together. It was one of the reasons she'd left things alone and hadn't disturbed Leni's life. She knew they loved each other and didn't want to take Leni away from her cousin."

"You say she approached Mani about Leni?"

"That's what she said. That he'd told her about his plans to get involved with the gang and then work it out with Sergio to eventually step in. By then, he'd have secured Leni's release, and Sergio had agreed Mani could walk away too."

"Now, after her lunch with Flossie, Leni believes Sergio is the killer, and she's hardwired to go after him. Goddamn. That's a tough one. No wonder my poor girl's been half crazy lately. I guess we have to warn Sergio, and then as soon as we get Leni alone, we have to get her head straight."

"I already called him earlier. He promised to be careful." Cassi stared at Mike, fear obvious in her worried expression. "Maybe I should have just blurted it out when you guys first got here, but I didn't want to mess with her too much before she saw the news. Poor Leni. Sometimes shit does come in waves."

Chapter Twenty-thre e

"Are you going to say something?" Lorraine's weak voice wobbled. "Ask me where I've been all your life, call me names... yell?" Lorraine flung herself towards the chair she'd occupied the day before. "I need to sit down before I fall. My knee is screaming."

Leni followed her into the room but refused to take a seat. Instead, she stood with her arms crossed and leaned against the doorway. "Tell me."

"Tell you what? That I've regretted giving you up every day of my sad, sorry life. I have. That I watched you from afar when I should have been the one you ran to when you came home from school rather than my brother. I did. That living in danger, doing good in the world and giving up any chance of happiness or having a family and moving on satisfied the guilt I've carried. It didn't. When I was eighteen, full of anger at my lover and making decisions I had no right making, thinking like a child rather than an adult, I made a horrible mistake and it's always been too late to fix it."

"Like you ever wanted to."

"Oh, trust me, Arlene. Oh, sorry, that's how I've always thought of you. Leni. You can't begin to understand how easy it is to shut off your brain and make stupid choices from a dark place of hate and hurt. That's how José made me feel before you were born. I never forgave the man, and so I couldn't move on. By the time I'd seen the light, it was too late. The times I'd gotten enough backbone to approach you and try to make amends, I saw you with Mani or my brother and you looked so happy. I took the easy way out and backed down, told myself it was in your best interests, but I was a coward. I guess I should have found the courage to approach you at Mani's funeral, but I was frightened that the shock would make Phil worse. I knew he was dying, and I just couldn't do it."

"You're a CIA agent. You fight the tough guys, probably carried a gun and used it – saved the world from terror. And, you couldn't bring yourself to talk to a little girl?"

"No, I couldn't bring myself to rip that precious little girl from the only home she'd ever known, a cousin she loved, the man she'd made her daddy and a life of safety to go to a world where her mother was always away. Where there were animals who might have used her daughter to get back at the agent who'd made a lot of enemies."

Leni took each hit to her heart and soon she couldn't see from the tears flooding her face. She slowly approached Lorraine who sat as if transfixed. "You did care." She sat close but didn't reach out.

"Yes. I loved you enough to give you a good life. Or that's what I told myself. Sometimes the devil hovering around whispered that I was a coward. And I've learned to believe in that truth also. I'm so very, very sorry, Leni. For you losing Mani and then Phil. What a lot of suffering you've gone through. I wished I could have been there for you. I'm just so thankful you still have Barb."

Unwilling to share that Barb and her just recently found the way to each other after a lifetime of dysfunction, Leni changed the subject and asked, "You talk about Mani as if you knew him. He was the best cousin in the world, and he shouldn't have died. The man who killed him is walking around free today, and that sucks so bad, I can hardly stand it."

"Are you sure? My information says differently. That Sergio Mandalas, the gang leader of the man who killed the people at the club, had him convicted."

Leni's disgust grew. "He set up someone to take the fall for his own crime. The prick needs to pay."

She shot to her feet and headed toward the door. Lorraine's voice stopped her. "Where are you going?"

"To finish this once and for all."

"Leni, finish what? We need to talk more. You have to understand that your reputation is going to be put through the wringer."

"Not so, mother dearest. You'll be the one with questions to answer, not me. I'm the innocent child who never even knew if her mother was alive or dead."

A cry escaped from Lorraine; one she couldn't hide in time. "You're right. Of course, you're right."

Leni stopped, her back to her mother. "That was uncalled for, Lorraine. Look, I'm in a bad place right now. But when everything has calmed down, we'll talk again."

Then she left the room and headed for her car, the tires squealing as she pulled away from the curb.

Chapter
Twenty-four

Leni knew where Sergio was bound to show sooner or later, and she hoped if she hung around long enough, she'd be lucky today. Sitting in a rental car across from Sam's Club, she watched for the Hummer that would mean Sergio had arrived.

After she'd left Cass's house, she'd driven home to get the bundle of cash she always kept in the safe for emergencies. Then she dropped her car off in an underground parking lot and headed to the nearest car rental agency to get wheels that wouldn't be identified. She'd known how Mike had found her the night before, and she didn't want that to happen again. This time she needed to be on her own. No way she wanted him to get into trouble because of what she needed to do.

She'd also fetched his secondary weapon from the safe while she had it open. Knowing it might come in handy, she hid it in the back of her jeans and slipped a light black leather jacket on to cover it up.

Waiting in the car, she replayed the words Lorraine had shared earlier. Though she now believed her mother hadn't been the callous bitch she'd tried to make her into, she still held her grievances close.

She'd meant to ask her about Mani and had forgotten to get that bit of information. Shit! That had been the whole reason she'd agreed to be in the same room with the woman in the first place. How could she have forgotten? Everything happened too fast. They'd talk again, and next time, she'd listen.

One minute, she was making plans, and the next she was crying so hard she could scarcely breathe. Staying down low in the SUV, she let it all out. The rage she'd been living with for years, always hovering close to the surface, always ready to pop out when she least expected to lose control. It had made her life miserable so many times, the lousy anger and hate she felt... for the world, for God who'd played such a horrible trick on her and... Jesus! For herself.

Oh my God. It was true. She didn't hate the world. It was her she hated. Her she blamed because her mother had left. Her she blamed because spoiled and foolish, she'd run away from people who loved her to get involved with a gang full of criminals and misfits. So that Mani, her beloved Mani, had sacrificed himself and his future to save her. How could she go on, carrying this burden?

Christ. How could she not? The words came out of nowhere but rang with truth. How could she leave Mike and Barb and everyone who loved her? How could she break the law, then bring a criminal to justice because she wanted it to be that way? Where did she get off thinking herself so powerful that she could kill in cold blood if forced? Remembering the last time her finger had been on the trigger of the gun that had killed her half-brother, Leni felt a wave of sickness. She grabbed for the water bottle to wash it down.

The heat in the parked car turned it into a furnace so she opened the windows to catch the small breeze so unusual in Vegas. Smells of scorched pavement and exhaust fumes had her change her mind. Instead, she reached to turn on the air conditioner to cool off the interior until she felt human again.

Relaxed, her brain fired messages so quickly that it overloaded all the circuits. Unaware it would happen, Leni dropped off into a sleep of necessity, almost as if she lost consciousness. Hours passed while she dozed, and when she finally woke up, darkness had descended. Stiff, her neck sore, she rubbed at it, angling it every which way to get the blood circulating again. She glanced around her and saw that the club across the road had a parking lot full of cars, including the souped-up Hummer she'd been on the lookout for.

Now what? Did she still intend to wreak havoc with the man? Acknowledging the truth, that she had no intention of killing anyone and had finally put that demon to bed, she still wanted answers to some of her questions. Maybe that would give her the peace she needed to move on.

Leaving the safety of the vehicle, she headed toward the club entrance and saw the glowing signs all over the outside of the old-fashioned pub-like building. The biggest sign that read "Pool Tables" flashed from the front window where inside she could see the milling customers laughing, drinking, filling the booths and many at the tables. She waited and watched, trying to build her courage to face whatever Sergio had to say.

As she stood there, she heard voices from around the side of the building and sensed there were a group of men rather than just a couple. The hair on the back of her neck began to stand up. Instinct from the days with the gang rushed in, and she knew without a doubt that something nefarious was being planned, and if she entered, she'd likely be caught smack dab in the middle.

Slipping into the shadow of the wall, she inched closer to where she could hear what was being said.

"You sure you want to take on Sergio Mandalas, Justin? He's surrounded by bodyguards, man. The last guy who tried challenging him ended up in a jail cell with a ten-year sentence."

"Shut the fuck up. If you're not with us, now's your chance to leave. Once we enter the club, the shit's gonna fly and only one of us will be alive to take over... be top dog. And, I intend that to be me. Does Jess have the rifles?"

Not staying to listen to more, adrenalin so rampant that it was hard to put one foot in front of the other or keep her mind clear, Leni crept back to the front of the building and hesitated. Pulling on the same resources she used in the ring when confronted by danger, she skimmed her choices. Did she leave and let the bricks fall where they may? Or, did she warn Sergio and his people so they might be able to escape or at least protect themselves?

Taking a few extra seconds to send Trace and Mike a text, she made up her mind. The door closed behind her as she scanned the room to see the man she'd been looking for playing pool at a back table. Just as she found him, his eyes lifted and registered recognition. As if on guard for just this type of occurrence, Doug stepped in front of Sergio until he saw it was her in the entrance. Then he relaxed his protective stance.

Sergio waved her forward, and the rest of the bar's occupants opened a pathway so she could approach. Instead of closing the gap – like one playing charades – she motioned with her hand that there was danger on the left side of the building. He came at her quickly and pulled her aside so she wouldn't be in the open. "What's up, Leni. Cass said some stupid shit about you gunning for me. What's with that?"

"No, it's not me. There're men gathered outside the building with rifles. They intend to attack any minute. You've got to escape, get out a window or something. They want to kill you and take over the gang."

"Oh, shit. Not again. Doug, get the boys. We're leaving. Leni's coming with us."

Before they could move, four men crashed in through the front door and the bullets began to fly. Sergio, moving his body to shield hers, pulled her behind the bar, using the small fridge for added protection. The mirror above shattered, the glass exploding all around them. He put his hand over her head and tucked her close to his side.

Reaching for his weapon, he came up empty-handed. "Fuck, I left my gun at the table so I could play pool. Stay low, sweetheart, I'll be back."

"No, you'll get shot. Don't go. Here I have a gun, use mine."

"Where'd you get that?"

"It's Mike's."

"Not a good idea for Kowalski's weapon to be found at a gang crime scene. Keep it for your own protection."

Before she could argue, she saw the barrel of a rifle aimed at them. Not thinking, just reacting, she lifted her weapon and pulled the trigger. It all happened so quickly, one minute they were under siege and fighting for their lives, and the next thing they heard was a loud male voice, screaming for Sergio to come out or Doug would be killed by the gun they had pointed at his head.

"No. They'll kill you." Leni saw the man getting ready to stand up.

"Or they'll kill Doug. He's not the boss, I am. It's my place, Leni. Honey. It's okay."

Just as he started to get to his feet, Leni heard the sirens in the distance and prayed they'd get there in time. Then she pushed Sergio, so he fell backward, his head hitting the edge of a box and stood with her hands in the air.

Shitting herself came close to describing the emotions she suffered, but it was the only way she could think of to give them the precious minutes they needed before help arrived.

"He's not here. He got away before you came in." The quiet in the building was eerie, as if no one could believe their eyes to see Leni and not the one they expected.

Terrified she'd see dead bodies all over, relief soared when she only saw a few wounded, holding their blood-soaked bodies to stem the flow. The earlier filled-to-capacity bar was now basically empty except for Sergio's gang members and the assailants who'd come to wreak havoc.

The man with the voice she recognized, the one

they called Justin, stood next to Sergio's bodyguard, his gun pointed at Doug's head. "You're lying, bitch. The man's hiding behind you, the fucking chicken-livered son of a bitch."

"You think so?" Sergio's voice, full of gravel and meanness, rang out as he suddenly appeared. They watched as Justin moved to put Doug between them. "Ahhh... not so fucking brave now are you?"

Even though she'd tried to protect him, Sergio would have none of it. Struggling to stay upright, blood pouring out of the wound on his head from where she'd pushed him, he grabbed at her to try and force her back down for protection.

She struggled, and he was forced to give up.

"Fucking prick. Did you have to shoot up the place and hurt all these people so you could prove what a big man you are? Jesus! I'm so sick of you wannabes always thinkin' you can be the boss, take over my boys. It ain't gonna happen, dude. They go with whoever they want to. By the way, you'd better let Doug go 'cause you're pissin' him off, and he's likely to blow."

Nerveless, Sergio staggered out from behind the bar, a small-built man, muscles in every part of his body, brave in the line of fire, his gaze dead cold to the ones who feared him. Leni saw it all, how he could control the others with just a look, why they followed him, the reason for the respect men twice his size showered on him. He was a born leader.

On the other hand, Justin's sick excitement

could be seen by everyone, a man who had to build up his nerve with booze and drugs, get high with fake courage. He turned his gun toward Sergio. Before he could fire, three things happened at once. Leni dove at Sergio to push him to safety. Doug's wicked backhand whipped the murdering asshole halfway across the room. And Mike's furious call rang out. "Stop where you are, Fuckies. LVPD."

Chapter
Twenty-five

Leni couldn't believe it when Cass came from behind the police officers traveling with Mike and Trace and flew at her, an expression of fury mixed with fear on her face. She crouched beside Leni; her voice full of relief to see she was alive. "You're bleeding. Where're you hurt?"

"I'm not. It's Sergio's blood."

The man who lay under her, shuffled her gently aside so he could stand, then he helped her to her feet and steadied her so she wouldn't go down again. He pointed his finger at her, his voice low but biting. "I could kick your ass if I didn't want to kiss you instead. Man, you're some crazy chick, almost as bad as your sister."

Leni stood looking at Sergio and a memory shifted in from the past of him saving her and Cass from crazy Juan Acedo when he'd tried to take them hostage. She'd forgotten about that. "I came to talk to you."

"According to Cass, she warned me you had more than talking on your mind. You have some crazy idea that I killed mi amigo, Mani. You're wrong. I didn't. But I might have been somewhat responsible for that shooting, and for that I'm sorry. I didn't know the boys would go loco and shoot up the Lipstick Club that night for retaliation. They felt justified because Gregorio Mende's two little girls were killed."

Leni stared at the man, into his eyes and saw the light of truth shining. The earlier, blood-curdling freeze evaporated slightly when he stared back at her. Then she saw something else appear when he turned to her sister. Warmth increased to adoration before he blinked and shielded the truth. *Ohhh...* She knew his secret. But it was his to reveal.

Mike suddenly spoke up from behind her where he'd stood back, watchful... protective. "You okay, baby?"

Leni turned to him and threw herself into his arms. She'd never been so glad to be alive. This night had proven one thing to her. After seeing that rifle pointed her way and knowing she could have died from a stray bullet, she'd realized that her life was a precious gift.

A memory surfaced, and she stood back. "Mike, I think I shot a guy who aimed his gun at Sergio and me when we were behind the bar."

Sergio stepped forward, his voice fierce. "Hey, lady, those are my fingerprints on the gun. Quit bullshitting your man that you shot anyone. It was me."

Trace approached and put a stop to their argument. "If you're arguing about the idiot who has some hair missing on the top of his head where – from his crazy babbling – he said someone shot him, and they missed by that much." He held his fingers up about an inch apart. "I don't think you have to worry. He's on his feet and bragging to anyone who'll listen to him about his close call. I guess the devil will have to wait for another day."

Sergio winked at her then, his relief obvious.

She smiled back, a lightness flooding her spirit that had been missing for far too long.

Then Leni turned to her sister, and it dawned on her that Cass had left the baby. "Where's Nico?"

"With Faith. No doubt she's fretting up a storm, so I'd better give her a call and tell her we're good." She stepped close to Leni and stared her down. "We're good now, right?"

Leni reached in for the hug she knew Cass would probably appreciate and whispered, "I won't speak for you, sis, but I'm fucking perfect."

Chapter
Twenty-six

By the time the police had gotten statements from everyone, and she was cleared along with Sergio and Doug who were the victims, Leni was heading outside and couldn't remember where she'd left her car. Then it came back to her how she'd gotten a rental and stalked a man with a crazy idea of inflicting punishment. Mike came to her side and pulled her into his embrace. "Where do you think you're going?"

"I was looking for my car, and then I remembered I had a rental."

"So, that's why we couldn't find any trace of you when we put out the APB on your license plates."

Shamefaced, she admitted, "I realized that's how you found me at the Lipstick Club, and I wanted to stay under the radar tonight. Mike, I was crazy with grief when I thought Sergio had shot Mani. I had it in my head to confront him, maybe shoot him, truthfully, I don't know. I think I wanted to force him to confess so he would end up behind bars. At least, I hope that's what I had in my head."

"Honey, if you had meant to kill the man, he'd be dead now. Instead, from what he told us, you saved him – twice. He's in your debt, and from now on, you'll have him in your corner no matter whatever happens in your life. Like he is with Cassi, he'll be for you."

"You know he loves Cass, right?"

"His business. I just know she'll never be in any danger as long as he's alive, him and Trace."

"And you and me."

"Right! We're all family now. And family takes care of their own. I heard Cassi asking you if you were good and you whispered your reply. I couldn't hear what you said. Can you tell me?"

"I told her I was perfect. And I am. I have you to love, a family who cares, including a long-lost mother, and dear friends to be with. What more can a girl ask for?"

He kissed her gently, the longing in his lips sending her heart in a spin. "I know what you can ask for?"

Smiling at him, into his twinkling eyes, she said, "What's that?"

"A wedding ring on your finger and a baby in your arms."

Laughing softly, she nodded. "Can we reverse the order and start on the baby tonight?"

"Only if you finally agree to start organizing the wedding as soon as possible."

"Jesus, man. You're determined to get that band on my finger."

Laughing, he swung her into his arms and headed with her towards his vehicle. "You got it, baby. Okay, let's go home and make a little play friend for Nico."

The End

Afterword

Thank you so much for reading the 5th book in Her Sweet Revenge Series, *Faith*.

I loved writing this story and I hope you enjoyed reading it. Because I couldn't help myself, I had to follow up on the other heroine in this series, Arlene – the girl we all know as Leni. Her book can also be found on Amazon **mybook.to/SweetLeni**

If you did like this book, I would ask you for a favor. Wherever you purchased it, please take a few minutes and leave an honest review. Authors enjoy hearing that readers like their stories, and hopefully, others will read your words and choose to buy the book because of your sentiments. My website at **http://mimibarbour.com** now has all my books listed with links to the various publishers to make it easy for you to return to where you bought the book and to find my other work.

While you're there, I'd really appreciate it if you would sign up for my newsletter so I can keep in touch. http://bit.ly/mimibarbournewsletter

I normally send out newsletters every few months and you have my word that your address will never be shared.

Hugs, Mimi

Special Agent Murphy

Undercover FBI Book #8

by
New York Times Best-selling author,
Mimi Barbour

AMAZON
~*~*~

It's Christmas in Washington, but not for one heartsick family

Agent Shane Murphy has a hard time believing his life could get so crazy. Because of a choice – one he'd make again – he loses his superiority in the FBI. Now he's forced to work surveillance with a rookie female yapper. And... gets caught up in the kidnapping of a sixteen-year-old that pulls at the heartstrings he keeps hidden.

Fighting the budding attraction for his new partner, he stresses his way through an escalating nightmare. How can he be so infatuated with a trouble-magnet female who drives like a granny and isn't able to hide her sensitive reactions when on the job?

Agent Kathleen Edwards does a lot of things her new partner dislikes, but what's a girl to do when a man ties her in knots and turns her into a chatterbox. Working to uncover the mystery of who kidnapped the Senator's daughter, and where they're holding her, continuous conflicts arise.

Working alongside an attractive realist whose high morals make him someone to live up to,

Kayti's heart doesn't stand a chance.

Dedication:

My late husband's persona is the heart and soul for Special Agent Murphy. While bringing out some of his most endearing and stubborn characteristics, his favorite cuss words and his way of looking at the world, I found myself falling in love with the wonderful man all over again.

Together Forever, my love.

Praise:

"I enjoyed this story! It's a good addition to the "Undercover FBI" series of stand-alone stories. Passion ignites between partners. I love the characters and the plot is intriguing. It's entertaining and a good mix of action, suspense, passion, and romance. I look forward to reading what this author comes up with next." ~ **Reviewed by Mary**

"This is a great series! Great characters in each book and a storyline you'll love reading. Special Agent Murphy is a great addition to the series. You'll love the characters, the storyline is enjoyable to read and very well written."~ **Reviewed by buzymomof2**

"This book was so good and I have really been loving this series! Murphy and Kayti made such an amazing team, in and out of the field, and I loved that they seemed like an opposites attract couple with some amazing chemistry! Murphy is loyal, hard-working, shows a crusty side, but has a huge heart! And I really loved his protective nature when it came to those he loved. Kayti has a huge heart, a softer touch with those in need, but loved how she was like Wonder Woman when it came to kicking butt and wanting to protect others! I loved the case that they were assigned to, full of drama, mystery, and danger! This was a great romantic suspense book and I look forward to more from Ms. Barbour!" ~Reviewed by Jessica N

Chapter One - Special Agent Murphy

Murphy pulled into his driveway and saw his neighbor acting like an asshole again. It happened often, and Murphy was sick of it. He left the car, intending to ignore the fact that the kid was getting blasted.

"Little shit. You listen to me when I talk to you."

"When you make sense, maybe I will. Until then, back off and leave me alone. I'm not handing over any money, so give it up."

"I feed you, clothe you and put a fucking roof over your head. Then, when I ask for a few bucks, you act like I'm some mysterious thief trying to steal your future. Piss on your future, what about now? What about me? I need money."

"Then get off your lazy fat ass, get a job and earn some – like you've made me do."

Losing his shit, the older man suddenly turned into a crazy fool. He rushed at the boy, grabbed him by his arm and hauled back to punch. In earlier years, no doubt, he'd have connected, but now the boy was strong and filled with angry disgust. Rather than take the punishment, he yanked himself from the other's grasp, turned and started to leave.

Only he didn't see his dad pull off the piece of broken fence, whip it behind his back and swing full force.

If Murphy hadn't stepped out at that moment to haul the kid away, the board would have connected, and no doubt would have done some damage.

He pointed at his door, pushed the kid in the direction and growled, "Get into the house. Now!"

Once Talin had disappeared, he pulled the drunk to his feet – the force from his wild swing having landed him on his ass – and shook him like a rag. "Campbell, you're a disgrace to the male race and fatherhood."

"The brat disrespe-ched... me."

"That makes two of us." He pushed the man toward his open back door, "Chrissakes, get out of my sight before I give you what you've got coming. And have a shower, you stink like puke."

***

"Jesus, kid. What set him off like that?"

"He's drunk."

"He's always drunk."

"Yeah, well tonight he was a mean drunk."

"I heard him after you for money. You working?"

Talin went to the fridge and pulled out some

cheese, ham and bread. Next, he grabbed the frying pan from the cupboard and started putting together grilled cheese sandwiches, his favorite snack that surprisingly was always available for him at Murphy's place. "You want a couple?"

"Sure. What kind of job did you find?"

Talin stopped and looked up. Murphy drilled him with his no-nonsense look. "Hey, back off. I'm helping old man Whiteland two doors down clean his yard."

"Okay. Good. Don't look at me that way."

"You don't trust me to keep out of trouble? I'm hurt."

"Bullshit. There's assholes out there who'd like to have a youngster like you on their payroll, selling all kinds of shit. You know what I mean."

"I know. They've already approached me. I told them like you said. That you lived next door and would be on them quicker'n they could call for their mamas if they messed with me. Funny, they haven't come near since."

"Good. Keep your nose clean. Work the jobs you can do helping people around the neighborhood who can't do stuff for themselves. Keep it up and you'll get to college one day."

"Like you, I want to be in criminal justice."

"Not like me. It's a shit job. Most guys at work can't keep a family together and are always broke."

"I was talking the law side, like a lawyer."

"Yeah, well before you start deciding your

future, check with technology to see whether lawyer jobs will still be plentiful down the road."

"People will always break the law."

"True. Criminal attorneys might be around."

Murphy fixed his rye and coke and took the first swill, moaning from the good taste.

Talin watched and grinned. "How come you never get drunk from that stuff?"

"'Cause, I know my body. When to quit before I lose control. And don't say you want to be like me in that way too. It's my one vice, otherwise I'm perfect." A cynical grin broke out over a face not used to smiling."

"Last time I asked, you called it a crutch."

"Guess I'd had my second by then. Listen, squirt, grab a life where you don't need anything but brains and hard work."

"No more with the squirt bullshit. I figure I've outgrown that nickname."

"Fine, Batman, have it your way. Where's my dinner?"

Talin plated the four sandwiches and scored a big glass of milk from the fridge. "I'm staying tonight, okay?"

"Hell, yeah. I wouldn't ask a dog to go back next door the way your old man is tonight. I'll go and mess with him in the morning and see if I can't get him cleaned up."

"You're the only one he listens to anymore."

"That's 'cause I scare the shit outta him."

Murphy took another long swill. "He's an idiot, but not a complete loss. Your mom's death hit him hard."

"Maybe you should tell him what you told me."

"What's that?"

"You growled at me when I was being pathetic. You said, she'd hate to see me become a loser and use the excuse of her dying to behave like a shit. But, if I used her memory to become the son she'd be proud of, she'd be smiling with the angels. Remember?"

"Yeah. It's good advice. Don't know how I got so smart." Murphy chuckled.

Talin pulled a funny face and took a huge bite.

***If you'd like to continue reading this story, click here for my Amazon Universal link: http://mybook.to/SpecialAgentMurphy

***This book is free in Kindle Unlimited.

Author, Mimi Barbour

NYT & USAT Best-selling, award-winning author

Mimi is an incredibly busy New York Times, USA Today and award-winning, best-selling author who has nine series to her credit.

She lives on the beautiful east coast of Vancouver Island and fills most of her day with writing and promoting her work. The rest of her time is spent in her garden, doing minimal housework and planning weird meals to ward off starvation.

"The favorite part of my job is meeting the characters from each new book. Creating them the way I want and having them act however I think they should. It's thrilling. Especially when most of my make-believe folks are interesting, witty and in most cases, people I would love to know."

Contact me

Write to me, I truly love hearing from my readers!

~ ~

My website: http://www.mimibarbour.com/
Follow me on Twitter, Facebook, Pinterest
Amazon, Goodreads, BookBub, LinkedIn